THE SECRET OF THE POISON RING

AN OUTLANDS ADVENTURE

DOROTHY
YOUNG
CROMAN

WindRider B O O K S
Tyndale House Publishers, Inc., Wheaton, Illinois

Other Books by Dorothy Young Croman

The Mystery of Steamboat Rock
Danger in Sagebrush Country
Trouble on the Blue Fox Islands

First printing, April 1986
Library of Congress Catalog Card Number 85-51986
ISBN 0-8423-5898-6
Copyright 1986 by Dorothy Young Croman
Printed in the United States of America

*In memory of
Grandmother Stender Young who
came to America in 1862 when
she was fourteen years old.*

CONTENTS

O N E

PAPA'S
SURPRISE

It was October in the Big Bend country of eastern Washington Territory in the year 1886. Three miles from the Standar cabin the huge landmark called Steamboat Rock loomed up in the middle of the Grand Coulee which ended near the rushing Columbia River. This part of the Territory was also known as Columbia River Basin.

In the cabin two miles from the rim of the Coulee, two young sisters were seated at the long kitchen table now cluttered with their activities.

Their mother, humming softly, was stirring navy bean soup with salt pork and onion as it slowly simmered on top of the big range. In a nearby black iron kettle some chicken was gently stewing. Mama's golden brown hair was piled high on her head, and the moist heat from the kettles was causing ringlets to make a narrow frame for her oval-shaped face.

Older sister Carolyn looked up from an arrangement of dried twigs, weeds, and leaves she was making into a small yard for a little ceramic lamb. Impatiently, she tossed one of her long brown braids over her shoulder.

"I wonder how long Papa will be away," she said to no one in particular. "It's been almost a week now."

Frances, six years going on seven, gave a squeal and looked up from the slate lying before her. She had been drawing pictures with the stub of a colored chalk. Her soft golden hair was in turned-up braids, with pert little blue bows tight against her head.

"He's coming now," she said. "Papa's coming!" She held her head to one side as she listened. "Can't you hear him?"

Just then their older brother, Eddie, tall and skinny (as Mama said), came into the cabin. He walked over next to Mama to warm his hands above the stove, then sniffed the air.

"Something smells good," he said, then added, "Papa's coming, singing a new song. Good thing he's here. It's turning colder and there'll be frost tonight; maybe even snow."

Then Carolyn did hear someone singing. She looked sharply at her little sister. How did she know? It was Papa all right. People said the Standars were a happy family because someone was always singing. Mama herself usually hummed or sang softly as she worked around the kitchen.

Everyone stopped to listen; then Frances jumped

to her feet. She ran to the wall where her coat was hanging. "I'm going to meet him," she said in excitement.

Carolyn smiled. Papa had made up a new song. His early morning songs sung while he was building a fire in the big range or the fireplace were often made up. By the time the cabin was warm and all were awake he always ended with, "Up, everyone. Time to get up!"

Carolyn leaped to her feet to follow Frances, flinging on her coat as she rushed out. Papa was singing now because he was glad to be home from the one-hundred-mile trip to Spokane.

The cold breeze carried in his ringing baritone:

> *Home is the traveler, like a sailor at sea,*
> *Home is the traveler, happy is he,*
> *Home is the traveler, weary with strain,*
> *Home is the traveler, no longer in pain.*
> *Home, home, sweet home,*
> *There is no place like home.*

Hand in hand, the sisters raced along the dusty road to meet their father. As they reached the wagon, now loaded with all kinds of supplies, he stopped the mules. The girls, long dresses under their coats tangling around their slim legs, climbed up. They each hugged Papa before he could drive on, and he squeezed them hard in return.

"Oh, Papa, we missed you!" cried Frances, giving his thick black beard a gentle pat. "I thought you would never come home. A weasel killed some chickens."

"I missed you too, Little Sister." He reached over and patted her head, then laughed. "What kind of a greeting is that?" To the mules he said, *"Giddap!"* He glanced at the older girl. "And how's my Carolyn?"

"I'm fine, Papa, but a weasel really did get into the chicken shed. It killed two of Mama's best Plymouth Rock hens before Eddie could get out to kill it. The squawking was awful. She said it got two of her best layers. You know how Mama feels about those hens. I'm sure she thinks as much of them as she does of us." Carolyn grinned. "Anyway, she made a stew and tonight we're having dumplings."

Papa flicked the reins over the black rumps of the mules. "Well, at least she didn't let the meat go to waste, regardless of how she feels. A stew is good. We'll eat less eggs if she wants to sell more. Then next spring we'll set more eggs to hatch out more chickens."

Again he flicked the reins over the rumps of the mules. "Has everyone been well?"

"Grandma has a little cold but she isn't really sick," said Carolyn. She smiled at the thought of her grandparents. Her mother had explained once that they were very special grandparents.

"Grandpa and Grandma have both been married before," Mama had said. "Grandpa's wife died, and so did Grandma's husband. In fact, Grandpa ia Papa's father, and Grandma is my mother."

"But—but Mama!" Carolyn remembered interrupting her in shock. "That makes you and Papa stepsister and stepbrother! Can you be married?"

Mama gave a little half-smile, her lips twitching in humor. "Well, we are, so it must be all right. Actually, your papa and I were already married and Eddie and you were born before our parents married each other. So you see, we aren't blood relatives. The word 'step' tells you that we are related only by the marriage of our parents, and that's nothing to hurt our own marriage."

It had taken Carolyn some time to adjust to this new information, but soon she realized it really didn't change anything.

Grandpa and his first wife had had four other sons, besides Papa. Carolyn enjoyed these uncles, who lived in another nearby cabin, across the spring and beyond her grandparent's cabin. Right now, the uncles were catching wild horses to build up a herd. They wanted to sell ponies to the continually arriving newcomers in their area.

"Has Grandma been taking care of herself?" Papa's question brought Carolyn's attention back to the present.

"She's been drinking bitter sage tea, and says it helps," she answered with a grimace.

"Good," said Papa. "If she drinks enough of that and takes plenty of quinine, she'll be all right."

"Ugh!" said Carolyn.

"Sometimes things that taste awful are good for us," said Papa quietly. By now they were at the cabin. Papa stopped the mules near Eddie who was waiting to take them to the big barn to unhitch and feed.

"Let's get this wagon unloaded first," Papa said, "then you can take them." He wrapped the reins around the long brake handle and jumped down.

The tired mules stood with heads drooping as Mama hurried out and threw herself into Papa's arms. He gave her a big hug as Eddie climbed up to hand down the packages.

"Louisa, I missed you! It's good to be home."

Mama did not say anything except, "Oh, Philip!" and gave him a kiss and a hard hug. Then she added, "A week is much too long to have you away."

Each child, along with Papa and Mama, took a package into the cabin, as Eddie was shoving some heavy things to the end of the wagon. He jumped down and carried a fifty-pound sack of flour inside where he dumped it near the cupboard next to the flour bin. He returned for a second sack while Papa carried a one-hundred-pound sack of sugar into the house.

"Philip! That's a lot of sugar!" exclaimed Mama.

"With Christmas coming I thought you might need some extra. The rest can always be used next summer for canning."

Christmas was still two months away but Carolyn knew that things like this had to be planned a long time ahead.

"I guess you're right," said Mama, picking up another package. "We'll be making Christmas cookies and pies and a plum pudding. But we'll also use some of that wild honey you found this fall."

Papa reached out to take the package from her, then changed his mind as he picked up two other bulky ones. He followed Mama into the cabin, said something to her, then they both went into their big bedroom and closed the door. Almost immediately they came out and Carolyn noticed that they did not have the packages.

The rest of the packages taken from the wagon were placed in one corner of the roomy kitchen. "We'll eat first and then open these," said Mama firmly. "Your father needs his supper."

By the time the wagon was unloaded, Carolyn had washed her hands and set the table. Mama was dishing up the food as Papa and Eddie each washed in the basin on a short bench near the door. A roller towel hung on the wall above the bench. A pail of water, with the handle of a gray dipper sticking up, sat at one end.

Mama placed a kettle of steaming stewed chicken and dumplings down in the center of the table as Carolyn was putting down a plate of baking powder biscuits. Mashed potatoes and some boiled turnips rounded out the meal. Glasses of fresh, rich milk stood at each child's plate, then Mama poured coffee for Papa and herself.

Mama had fixed something new—a small bowl of grated carrots. She placed them in the center of the table, then brought a small bowl of thick bean soup for each person to start the meal. She hung her black and white checked apron on a nail near the stove. Now everyone was sitting on the benches on each side of the long table. Papa had made rockers for Mama and himself, but had not yet taken time to make straight-backed chairs for the table. He would someday.

"Ummm, smells good," he said. "You can just bet I'm hungry! Nothing like your good cooking, Louisa." He glanced at the grated carrots. "What's that?"

Mama smiled. She liked to hear Papa say he liked her cooking. "Our supper didn't seem to have much color, so I thought some carrots might help."

"Raw?" Papa sounded doubtful.

"Yes, raw." She nodded firmly. "I didn't think of them in time to cook them. In the last Spokane paper was a new section on cooking and it said that raw vegetables are good for us."

Papa sort of grunted as though he was not at all sure that was true, but that bowl of orange-colored grated carrots did look nice sitting next to the white dumplings, potatoes, and turnips.

Now they all bowed their heads and folded their hands and Papa said, "Thank you, Lord, for this bountifully filled table. I thank you also for bringing me safely home to my loving family. Thou art ever mindful of our daily needs and thou daily giveth us many benefits. Amen."

After they finished eating, Papa said, "I think that weasel did us a good turn. That was a mighty fine supper." His dark eyes twinkled. "Even the raw carrots were good. And your dried apple pie was delicious."

Carolyn did not like even the thought of the hens

being killed by that nasty old weasel, but Papa was right. It was a particularly good supper.

As he finally pushed away from the table, he said, "I have a surprise for all of you."

"What, Papa, what?" Frances began bouncing on her toes.

The corners of Papa's mouth twitched. "I met Santa Claus in town, that's what."

"Santa Claus!" Frances' blue eyes became bigger and bigger. "Now? Christmas isn't here yet."

"You're right, it isn't, but I did meet Santa Claus! Come along, Little Sister. Sit on my lap and I'll tell you all about it."

He excused himself and they moved over to Papa's big rocking chair.

"What did he say, Papa?" She sounded breathless. "What did Santa Claus say?" The little girl could hardly sit still.

"Well," began Papa slowly, "he is beginning to check up on all the children to see if they are being good and helpful and kind. He said he couldn't get here last year because one of his reindeer went lame. He was sure he would make it this time. His reindeer are in much better condition now."

Carolyn and Eddie were wise as to who Santa Claus was, but the statement meant something anyway to all the family. They might have a Christmas tree, after all, and everything that went with it. They had had no Christmas their first year after arrival. There had been no extra money after that long, slow two-year covered wagon trip from Iowa.

Now Carolyn knew she would finish her dried weed arrangements, maybe for Christmas gifts. And she could begin to make some colored paper chains to decorate the tree. That would be fun.

Then Papa, pointing to the largest package he had placed on the floor in one corner of the room, said, "You may now open that package."

Frances jumped down, but Eddie beat her to the corner.

"Our shoes!" exclaimed Carolyn. "Our new shoes!"

Papa smiled and nodded as Eddie began tearing the paper from the package.

"Oh, don't tear it!" cried Carolyn. "I want to use that paper for drawing pictures."

"Waste not, want not," said Mama. "I want that string to put around my string ball. We never know when we'll be able to use such things."

"That's right, Son," said Papa. "Don't be in such a hurry that you can't save something useful. It may be needed later."

Eddie knew that but he was in such a hurry to get at those new shoes, he didn't care. During the summer the children went barefooted and, of course, by fall their feet had grown. Although they were long for her, Frances could wear Carolyn's hand-me-downs if they were not too shabby; but Eddie and Carolyn always had to have new shoes.

Finally the package was opened and there were the new black shoes with high button tops. This time even Frances had a new pair. They were heavy and clumsy but soon each child was listening to the squeaky sound the shoes made as he or she walked, watching their feet and admiring the shoes as something special. If they had been sandals of gold, the youngsters could not have been happier.

Mama stood up and started to ask Carolyn to clear the table, but one more package was to be opened. This time it was opened carefully, and both the string and the paper were saved and folded. In it were school supplies: pencils and crayons and writing paper for school assignments, a new slate for Little Sister so she would not have to use Carolyn's, and a brand new *Robinson's Arithmetic* book for the two older children.

Eddie was grinning as he opened the new book. "Thank you, Papa. I'll be careful with this." He looked at Carolyn. "We can take turns using it."

Sums would be harder in this book than the sums in the old one, but Carolyn knew that Eddie had to learn them before he could go to Courtland Academy, which was open to fifteen-year-olds. He would have to finish it, but she would work only in the first part of the book.

Papa wanted his children to be well-educated, but Mama was the one who drove them on. She insisted that education was the only way to get ahead. She remembered what a hard time she had had getting her education when she first arrived in America from Denmark. Her teaching certificate was one of her most valued possessions.

As Carolyn looked at their presents, her thoughts flew ahead to Christmas. Before the family had left

Iowa in 1881, getting ready for Christmas had been fun. Would it be the same here where they did not have so much to work with?

The first thing they had to do was to get ready for the Christmas entertainment at the schoolhouse during the first part of December. Eddie was to be in a play. Carolyn did not think that would be fun since she herself did not like to get up in front of a lot of people.

What *would* be fun was getting Frances ready to do her part. She had such long blonde hair and blue eyes, and was small for her six years. She had a clear little voice and could hold a tune nicely. Mama often helped her at the organ, as she was beginning to learn to play, but it was hard for her to reach the pedals to pump because her legs were so short. Carolyn also loved to help Frances sing.

The older girl could hardly get to sleep that night, thinking about the next two months until Christmas arrived. She sleepily wondered what was in the packages Papa and Mama had put in their bedroom, then smiled. This year promised to be a real Christmas celebration.

She had no way of knowing that Mama's first fourteen years in her native Denmark would begin to affect the family in Washington Territory in America before the winter was over. They would have much more to contend with than a Christmas celebration.

TWO
THE STRANGER

Eddie was right; Papa had reached home just in time. For the next week it snowed off and on; not a hard, blowing snow but a gentle, sifting snow that built up slowly. Both Papa and Eddie had worked hard to get plenty of wood cut and piled in the lean-to back of the cabin. Earlier they had shoveled much dirt around the base to keep out the cold.

They hoped the vegetables in the cellar underneath would not freeze. These had been grown during the summer, even though some of the neighbors said vegetables would not do well in this country. The barn was full of wild rye grass hay, with a big stack outside. Men interested in raising cattle and horses said that the land was not good for crops, but Papa did not feel that way. He said that next summer he would plant wheat and maybe some oats, and he certainly intended planting more vegetables.

In their little workshop in the barn Papa and Eddie had been making sleds. One was for the Hudson children. Now they were almost finished.

Robert David, nine years old, and his sister Sally Mae, now four, had come over with their mother from their new cabin on the other side of the spring to play with the Standar children. Mrs. Hudson was inside the house visiting with Mama. The baby, Merrilee, was only a year old and was just learning to walk.

The John Hudson family, originally from the South, had been in the area only a little over a year. At first they had trouble finding a place in which to live because they were black. Mama said that God meant for everyone to live together in peace. She had insisted that the Hudsons stay with them until their own cabin was built. Mr. Hudson had been helpful in tilling the land with Papa, and the children had all become good friends. The Hudsons had been in their own home, still rough, only since late fall.

The four children had been watching Papa and Eddie working on the new sled. Now the smaller children were becoming tired of watching. Frances suggested that they go outside and play in the snow.

Carolyn said, "Robert David, did you and Sally Mae ever make 'snow angels'?"

He looked up at her and shook his head, his dark eyes sparkling. "No. What are snow angels? We never even saw snow until now."

"Come on. You'll see." The children all went out of the barn.

The barnyard was clean and white and the snow

had stopped falling. Soft and loose, it was not over a foot deep. It was just right for falling into to make "angels."

Now Carolyn and Frances threw themselves down on their backs in the snow.

"Watch!" said Carolyn as Robert David and Sally Mae stood wide-eyed. "You move your arms up and down in the snow and your legs back and forth and you have snow angels."

Sure enough! After Carolyn and Frances each finished and stood up to move to another spot, they left figures in the snow that could be taken for angels.

Robert David and Sally Mae then threw themselves down on their backs and began making their own snow angels.

The children became so busy with their new activity, making angel after angel until a big space was covered, that they did not notice a man watching them.

Only when Carolyn sat up and started to say that she'd had enough did she notice the stranger snow-shoeing away from a corner of the barn. Puzzled, she stared at his retreating back. He turned his cap-covered head slightly and she saw he wore a scraggly, sandy-colored beard. He was tall and slim and moved as though the snowshoes were part of his feet. He probably was using them instead of skis because the snow was so new and soft.

Eddie, pulling the new sled, came from the barn a few minutes later. "This needs to be painted, but that will have to wait. Right now, with this new snow, the sled is needed. Here, Robert David." He reached the rope over to him. "You and Sally Mae may have this one."

"Oh!" exclaimed the boy. "For us to keep?"

Eddie nodded. "Yes, for you to keep for your very own, you and Sally Mae."

The little girl promptly sat down on it and looked at her brother, waiting for him to start pulling.

"Oh!" said Robert David again. "Thanks!"

"You're welcome," said Eddie, turning toward Carolyn as the two younger children began trying out their new sled.

"Eddie!" Carolyn could not keep quiet any longer. "Eddie, did you see that man?" She was looking toward the corner of the barn.

"What man?" Eddie looked around.

"I think he was standing over there at the corner watching us make snow angels. He left just as I sat up. He didn't say anything. He was on snowshoes, not skis."

Eddie, looking puzzled, went over to the corner of the barn. He looked down at the tracks and nodded. "You're right. A man did stand here. His tracks are going toward the Coulee wall."

"That man was taller than you," said Carolyn, "but I think he was a little heavier."

Eddie, now fourteen, was almost as tall as Papa but he was still very slim.

It was too late to follow the tracks. Eddie promised to do so the next morning, which was Saturday.

The children played with the new sled until all were tired and cold and wet. They went inside and warmed themselves until their mother was ready to leave. With Sally Mae sitting on the sled and Robert David pulling, they started for home, going by the barn to thank Mr. Standar.

Later, when Carolyn told her mother about the man, her mother was upset.

"I don't like it when strange men come around," she said, shaking her head. "You don't have any idea where he went?"

"No, Mama. I didn't see him until I sat up from the snow and then he was leaving. He was taller than Eddie but not as heavy as Papa."

At supper Carolyn told Papa about the man. He looked thoughtful and finally said, "We'll have to be on the lookout for a stranger. I want you children to be very careful. When the mail comes through we'll ask the driver if he has seen anyone in this area who seems suspicious."

Then he changed the subject. "There is one thing we'll have to do in the morning. Run that new rope I brought from Spokane from the cabin to the barn. This is blizzard country and when it blizzards it is easy to get lost just going from the cabin to the barn. I heard a number of stories in Spokane about how dangerous such weather can be. So we'll be ready for it."

Mama was more worried about the strange man than about blizzards. "You know, I can't help but worry when the children are out," she said. "One can't tell what a stranger will do."

"True," said Papa. "We'll ask God to watch over us. Our faith in him is a good protection, but we'll continue to be on the lookout." Again he stressed that perhaps the mail carrier might know something.

All was quiet for a few minutes, then Papa said, "How about some music tonight? I haven't heard any of you playing that organ for a while. Carolyn and Eddie haven't sung for us in a long time."

"I help Little Sister sometimes when you're out," said Carolyn. "She's learning to play."

Carolyn went over to the organ and began leafing through their songbook *Song King* by H. E. Palmer, a collection of songs originally put together in 1871. Mama had learned to play and sing them when she was young and now Carolyn was learning them. A number of songbooks had come with them by covered wagon over the long trail those two years they had traveled from Iowa. More than one song was sung on the trail when Mama felt like playing the little organ that stood in one corner of the mule-drawn wagon.

Now Carolyn came to the song "Have Courage, My Boy, to Say 'No.'" Her brown eyes began to twinkle as she looked at Eddie. Since he was going away to school next fall, this would be a good song to sing to him.

She did not say anything, just began to play and sing softly:

You're starting, my boy, on life's journey,
Along the grand highway of life.
You'll meet with a thousand temptations,
Each city with evil is rife.

This world is a stage of excitement,
There's danger wherever you go,
But if you are tempted in weakness,
Have courage, my boy, to say No!

Before she had gotten very far, Mama began singing with her, and then Papa. Eddie did not seem to know whether to join them or not, but finally when they began the chorus, he too joined in:

Have courage, my boy, to say No,
Have courage, my boy, to say No,
Have courage, my boy, have courage, my boy,
Have courage, my boy, to say No!

Eddie grinned. "I'll think about that," he said, reaching over to pull one of Carolyn's long brown braids.

They joined in singing the other two verses, then sang a long song called "Beautiful Home."

Carolyn wanted one more song so she and Little Sister could sing together. She quickly turned some pages and found "Value of Little."

"Little of what?" asked Eddie.

Carolyn ignored him. Instead she asked Frances

to stand near her. She knew her little sister could sing it because she often chimed in when Carolyn was practicing.

> *Do thy little, do it well;*
> *Do what right and reason tell,*
> *Do what wrong and sorrow claim.*
> *Conquer sin and cover shame.*
>
> *Do thy little, never fear*
> *While thy Savior standeth near;*
> *Let the world its jav'lins throw*
> *On the way undaunted go.*

Singing before going to bed made everyone feel good. Mama was happy and Papa looked satisfied.

Carolyn knew that tomorrow she would have to help Frances find a song to learn for the upcoming Christmas entertainment.

As she went to bed she began to think of the man who had been watching them playing in the snow. Just what did it mean? Did that man intend any harm?

Despite Eddie's promise to follow the tracks, that night it snowed again so no tracks of any kind could be seen the next day.

THREE
CHRISTMAS PREPARATIONS

Carolyn was looking through their many songbooks, trying to find a short song that Frances might sing for the Christmas program.

Frances was playing with a sleepy gray cat and now the cat turned away and curled up under a chair. That meant that tabby was tired of playing. Frances then went to the table where Carolyn had the books spread out, open to different pages as she searched for a song.

Suddenly Carolyn said, "Little Sister, look at this!" Her voice sounded excited. " 'Away in a Manger' is about the sleeping baby Jesus. Maybe you'd like to sing it.

"Martin Luther wrote it a long time ago. It says here, in 1530. My goodness, that's over 350 years ago! He started our Lutheran religion. Grandpa and Grandma will like this."

Time meant nothing to Frances but she was interested in the song.

Grandpa was a Lutheran minister and he took turns preaching with another one of the new settlers in the area.

The girls went to the organ and, with Frances standing at her side, Carolyn sat down on the round-topped stool. She pulled out some of the stops that helped to give the organ its fine tone. She looked at her little sister. "You listen and see if you like it."

Carolyn played the entire song without singing, then said, "It's a pretty tune. Now I'll sing the words."

Away in a manger, no crib for a bed,
The little Lord Jesus laid down His sweet head.
The stars in the heavens looked down where He lay,
The little Lord Jesus asleep in the hay.

Carolyn turned. "Do you like that? Do you think you would like to learn this for the program?"

Frances nodded. "Yes, I like that! Is there more?"

"Another verse," said Carolyn, as she went on:

The cattle are lowing, the baby awakes,
But little Lord Jesus no crying He makes.
I love Thee, Lord Jesus, look down from the sky,
And stay by my cradle 'til morning is nigh.

"What does 'nigh' mean?" asked Frances, looking at Carolyn.

"In this case I guess it means 'here' or maybe

'near.' Neither one rhymes with 'sky' so 'nigh' is used."

"What does 'lowing' means?" asked Frances.

"The cows are mooing softly to each other. You see, the baby Jesus did not have a bed such as you do. His mother put him in a manger and I guess the cows were telling each other what a beautiful baby he was. Would you like to learn the song?"

Frances nodded. "Oh, yes!"

From then until time for the Christmas program, Carolyn helped Little Sister to learn her song about the tiny Jesus. When Mama had time she also helped. She often hummed the tune or sang it while she was working and Frances would sing with her.

In the meantime Carolyn continued to make her weed and seed arrangements. She even had some petrified wood and some dried leaves of the Gingko trees one rider had brought up from the petrified forest to the south. Carolyn treasured them because Gingko trees did not grow as far north as their home.

She had a few cones from both the fir trees and pine trees that grew near the Coulee where Papa went for wood. She tried to save some of the branches but the needles fell off because they dried out too fast.

Leftover shingles cut in two, from when Papa and his brothers had shingled the cabin and the barn, made good bases for her various arrangements. Mama had shown her how to boil flour and water to make thick paste to hold everything in place.

Mama also taught her how to make dolls out of corn husks. Carolyn then tried to make little horses and cows, but it was hard to tell the difference between the animals. Putting horns on the cows was not easy.

One little figure that Carolyn treasured above all others was a small china sheep. It had been given to her by a neighbor woman who had, when she was a small girl, come in a sailing ship around Cape Horn at the southern tip of South America. Mama had been good to the family in helping them get settled. When Mrs. Fleet offered the little sheep to Carolyn in payment, Mama hesitated in letting her keep it, but Mrs. Fleet insisted.

Carolyn loved it and was very careful with it. Now she was making a special arrangement in which to place the sheep.

Some of the weeds were easy to work with. Cheat grass made graceful little branches with other plants, but the prickly seeds stuck to anything that touched them, like stockings or long dresses.

Teasel was interesting but the dried flower heads were prickly. Carolyn did not know the name of a plant that had tiny stars after it was dry. Wild poppies dried nicely, and dried white yarrow flowers were like upside-down umbrellas. Dried yarrow stems were straight and firm. Mama sometimes made tea of the flowers but it was so awful tasting no one really liked it.

Baby's breath made little clouds of dried white flowers, adding softness to stiff weeds. The strawflowers kept their colors of red and yellow after drying, giving color when mixed with other dried weed combinations.

Watching Carolyn one day, Mama said, "Those are nice, but why don't you let that go for a while and begin popping corn and stringing some for Christmas. We'll use it for decorations."

"Oh, Mama, what kind of decorations?" Carolyn looked up.

Mama smiled. "You'll see. But we'll need quite a bit and if you start now it won't seem so hard to get ready. You children can string the popped corn on some of that thick waxed thread I keep for extra heavy sewing." She reached out and touched the little sheep standing near a fence made of small sticks zigzagging across the shake shingle.

"Nice," she said softly, rubbing her forefinger over the back. "I'm going to begin making candles and I'll use some string from my string ball for wicks. How would you like to make popcorn balls, using a little of our wild honey? It will be messy, I'm afraid, but we don't have any maple syrup."

So corn popping began. Even Eddie and Frances helped, although at first they ate almost as much popcorn as they strung onto the heavy thread. Papa had brought a good supply of the unpopped corn from Spokane so they felt they would have plenty. Next year they might try to grow and dry their own.

When Thanksgiving came, it was a day to be particularly thankful for all the nice things that had happened since they had settled in eastern Washington

Territory. But soon it was over, and then it was time to think of Christmas and the program.

Carolyn knew that the Hudson family, as well as the grandparents and the four uncles, would all be included in this Christmas dinner. Mama had cared for two young geese all summer and would save the lovely soft down feathers for new pillows. She would roast one goose and Grandma the other and each would prepare some of the vegetables. Using a recipe she brought from Denmark, Grandma would make a special plum pudding and Mama would make mince pies. It would be a fine dinner.

In all the excitement of the coming entertainment and the Christmas preparations, everyone forgot about the man that Carolyn had seen the day she and the younger children were making snow angels.

Then at supper one evening Papa said, "I think one of our new neighbors saw the man you told us about, Sister. Eddie and I were near the Coulee today and met two of the Rusho boys. Chris told me that a man tried to question them as to who lived in our cabin. He said the man wouldn't give his name or where he was living. It seemed rather odd since usually everyone is so friendly."

Mama said, "Philip, do you think that man is dangerous? I mean, could he harm any of us in any way—particularly the children?"

Thoughtfully, Papa pulled at his thick beard. "That's exactly what I don't know. Chris couldn't give me any real information." He looked at Carolyn again. "Did you see his face at all?"

She shook her head. "Not really. He had his back to me when I first saw him. Then he turned his head a little and I caught a quick glimpse of the side of his face. He was wearing a full beard, but it was sort of scraggly, sandy color, not a nice heavy black one like yours."

Papa smiled at the "nice heavy black one like yours." He said. "Ummm, a sandy-colored beard, eh? That should help."

He finished eating and added, "I'll get the boys onto his trail if possible."

The "boys" were Papa's younger brothers, Adolph and Will and Jake and Louie. If anyone could find out about the stranger, certainly they should be able to. They spent a lot of time catching wild horses and looking over the big, wide open country around the Columbia River flowing not far from the Grand Coulee Canyon. New people coming into the area always wanted horses.

F O U R

SURPRISE MAIL

Carolyn, still working with her weed arrangements in between helping Little Sister learn her song for the Christmas program, reached for her little pottery lamb. Then she held her hand suspended.

Someone was coming. Men's voices sounded, the door burst open, and Papa and Mr. Long, the mail carrier, entered. A few flakes of snow swirled in behind them.

It was always fun when the mail carrier came. Ever since Papa had set up the Lincoln County Post Office at their place, the coming of the mail would mean visits from neighbors both near and far. People who came from very far away often stayed overnight, and Mama liked the extra money paid by most overnight guests.

"Hello, everyone!" cried Mr. Long, a short,

heavyset man with a heavy brown beard. "Wasn't sure I was going to make it this time. Not much snow here, but out toward Cottonwood the snow is deep and badly crusted over. Hard on horses' legs. It's good to be inside."

Papa looked at Eddie and said, "I put his horses inside the barn. They need food and water."

Mama picked up the gray enameled coffeepot that always stood at the back of the stove and started pouring black coffee into a mug. She set it down on the table.

"Sit down, Mr. Long, and warm yourself. Hope you've brought lots of mail. How did you find the traveling?"

Mr. Long took off his heavy macintosh and hung it on a peg near the door, then walked over to the table.

"Thank you, ma'am." He took up the mug of coffee and cradled it in both hands. "Feels good. Traveling's rough right now. Before the winter is over it'll be rougher. I may have to ride horseback instead of using the stagecoach. If the snow crusts over any more it's going to be hard to drive a team through. The crust cuts their legs. It'll be hard on cattle and horses out on the range, too. Heavy crust makes it impossible for horses or cows to paw through and reach the bunchgrass they eat during a milder winter. Range cattle starve in times like these."

Carolyn, listening to the men talk, wondered what would happen to their own cows. Papa had tried to keep the milk cows near or in the big barn or corral, but it was not possible to keep them there all the time. That big stack of feed in the barnyard would not last if this continued for very long. The younger stock ran free where they usually could forage.

"Are you using those leather boot tops laced around the horses' front legs yet?" asked Mama. "As I recall, you used them last year."

"Yes, I did," said Mr. Long, "but so far I've managed without them. I will use them if the crust on the snow gets worse."

Mama set down a plate of warm cinnamon rolls to go with the coffee. Mr. Long thanked her gratefully.

As soon as Papa and Mama had gone through their mail, which was not much this time, Papa began to talk about the man who had watched the children and the fact that no one seemed to know anything about him.

Mr. Long looked thoughtful. "You know, I think that may be the same man who has been wandering around Spokane. He has a full, light sandy-colored beard. He hasn't hurt anyone that I know of but people do wonder about him. When was he here?"

Carolyn spoke up. "It was the week after it began snowing." She told about how she and the younger children had been making snow angels, but had not noticed the man until they were ready to come back into the cabin.

Mr. Long tapped the table with one finger. "Ummm, very odd. If it was the same man in Spokane, I wonder how he made that trip. He didn't go in with me. Maybe someone else took him, or maybe he rode horseback. That's a slow, tedious, cold trip." Again he looked thoughtful as he slowly sipped his coffee and ate another cinnamon roll.

Everyone was silent. Then Eddie returned to the cabin, followed by two of the nearby neighbors who had come to pick up their mail. Papa was now busily sorting it all into cubbyholes in his small office.

While the men were talking, Mama had been glancing over the new *Spokesman Review.* Suddenly she gave an exclamation, "Listen, everyone! This may be our man." She read a few more words. "I can't believe it!"

Finally she looked up, then down again as she began to read slowly, "Ditlef Carsten, originally from Copenhagen, Denmark, has been making inquiries about a friend he has not seen for years and is not even sure is in this part of the country. If anyone knows the whereabouts of a family by the name of Standar, please get in touch with this paper."

She looked up, her blue eyes wide and questioning. "Philip, do you know anyone by the name of Ditlef Carsten?"

Papa shook his head. "You're from Denmark, not me. My people came from Germany. Louisa, he must mean you or your mother."

Mr. Long interrupted by saying he had to leave. He thanked Mama again for the coffee and cinnamon rolls and said he would get the rest of the story when he came through again. He would keep an eye open for the man. He told Papa he could get his horses. The other two men followed him out.

Mama hardly heard them as they left. She was reading the paper again, and she had turned white as her eyes took on a haunted look.

"It can't be!" she whispered. "It just can't be! Not after all these years." She looked up. "I had a cousin by the name of Herman Carsten and he was a scamp. I think he had a half-brother, Ditlef, who was much younger." She shook her head slowly.

"Herman asked me to marry him and I wouldn't. For one thing I was too young, only thirteen, and for another I had fallen in love with another man. Herman stole a large sum of money from my father. A thousand dollars it was. I think he did it to get even for my not marrying him." Mama took a big breath and let it out slowly. "We considered having him arrested, but that would have brought shame to the whole family. That is one reason we came to America. In Denmark we were quite well off. My father was a millwright and an architect. He had a gristmill, a big farm, and we had four servants. Then he lost everything because that money to pay off the mortgage was stolen." She seemed to be talking to herself.

Carolyn, her eyes bright, began to wonder what it would be like to have servants. Mama had never told them about this part of her life in Denmark, although she had said she was born way up north in a little place called Havens Molle in Horby Parish.

Mama looked over at Papa, and Carolyn wondered if she was going to cry.

"Forgive me, Philip. I don't want to hurt you because I love you now and am very happy with my fine family. Christian Hamilton and I fell in love. He also wanted me to marry him. I met him through my Aunt Cordelia who was lady-in-waiting to the Queen of Denmark. Christian had everything a girl could want, but his wife was already picked out for him. You see, he was a nobleman. I had just turned fourteen." She was thoughtful a moment. "I believe he had a younger brother, Jens, about my age."

Astounded, Carolyn stared at her mother. Mama in love with someone when she was only fourteen?

Her mother stopped talking and her eyes became dreamy as though she were looking into the past.

Frances went over to Papa and climbed into his lap. Looking at her young sister gave Carolyn a strange feeling. For the first time she noticed how much the child looked like Mama. She had fine, slender bones, with delicate hands that made her look like a Dresden doll. (Carolyn had never actually seen a Dresden doll but she had seen pictures of them in one of Mama's books.)

Even today Carolyn heard people talk about Mama's good looks, after having three children and working so hard. Little Sister had the same good looks, lovely blue eyes, creamy skin, and golden hair.

Mama looked at Carolyn. "I have been in America for over twenty years. I was fourteen years old, just a little older than you, when we arrived in New York." She shook her head. "There would have been no happiness for me in Denmark."

She walked over to Papa and put one hand on his left shoulder.

"Yes, my father lost his property, but I think part of the reason for our coming to America was to get me away from Christian. Papa had to make a new start, but he soon became ill."

"But, Mama," said Carolyn, "if you loved a man and he loved you, couldn't you wait until you were older to get married?"

She felt as though she were talking about a stranger, not her own mother.

Mama smiled. "Things don't happen that way with the nobility. I was a commoner, with no royal blood in my veins, and he was much older. It was time for him to marry. One day he said he could not see me anymore and gave me a ring so I would remember him. As if I could ever forget him! My heart was broken."

Carolyn stared at Mama. What would it be like to be in love with a nobleman and have her heart broken?

Mama said softly, "Christian's mother and father, Lady Hamilton and Sir William, were kind to me. But his mother made it very clear that we could never marry. It was a shock!"

Mama stood quietly for a moment, staring into the past. Was she wondering what might have been? Carolyn was quiet too—the fact that her mother, her very own mother, had been in love with another man besides Papa was a surprise.

Mama must have been pretty as a girl. When Carolyn was younger she remembered her mother used to wear little curls around her lovely oval-shaped face. Now she usually just combed her hair back and piled it on top of her head, although little wispy curls often came loose.

"There is one thing in connection with all this that I have never shown any of you." She stooped over and put her cheek against the top of Papa's head. "I still have the ring, a poison ring, that Christian gave me. He said it was the only possession that he could give me to remember him by. I have kept it all these years."

"A poison ring! What kind of a ring is *that?*" Carolyn could not imagine what a "poison ring" was like or what it was used for.

Mama now put her arm across both of Papa's shoulders and gave him a little hug. "You have given me a good life, Philip. Remember, I do love you, and only you."

Papa looked uncertain. "I'm not sure about that. I think I have given you nothing but a lot of hard work. Nobility? I didn't know your folks had any connection with nobility."

"We didn't, not really," said Mama. "Only through Aunt Cordelia as lady-in-waiting to the Queen. When we came to America even that slight connection was broken."

By now Papa had put one arm around Mama's waist, while the other was still around Little Sister who sat quietly in his lap.

Carolyn kept staring at her mother. Her life in

America had not been easy. Just driving that long, long way from Iowa in covered wagons with the rest of Papa's family over a two-year period was hard. But Mama was always cheerful and kind and happy, and took care of anyone who was sick. She herself never seemed to be sick. She insisted that cheerfulness was the best promoter of health, friendly to the mind as well as to the body. And one must walk with God, always walk with God to be happy.

"Mama, when may we see the poison ring?"

Mama still held the *Spokesman* article in her hand. She stood up straight, gave a big sigh, and said, "Oh, yes, the ring." She glanced down at the article again. "I'll show it to you later. Now we'll have to figure out how we are going to see this Ditlef and find out what he wants." She frowned. "I can't imagine how anyone connected with Herman has managed to find us or what he might want."

She took a big breath. "My, that was a stormy trip coming across the Atlantic Ocean in a sailing ship. Everyone was seasick except me. My mother and father were both down and I took care of everyone, even a little sister who later died from typhoid fever."

Mama brushed her hand across her forehead. It was as though she did not want to remember that long-ago period.

"Mama's sister, my Aunt Margaret, and her four children, were with us. It was Aunt Margaret who paid our way to America because we had nothing left after the money was stolen."

Papa got up slowly from the chair and said he was

going out. Carolyn suspected that he knew this part of the story.

Finally Carolyn said, "Mama, how did you happen to marry Papa? Where did you meet him?"

Mama was thoughtful for a few moments. Then, as though she had not heard the question, she said, "My father continued to be very ill after we reached New York. My mother stayed with him while my brother Edward, who was two years younger, and I went with Aunt Margaret and her children. She was going to Cresco, Iowa, to join her husband, Hendricksen, who had arrived earlier. A few weeks later my father died and my mother came to Iowa to join us."

Mama was silent for a long time. She shook her head slowly. "We had a rough time. I found a place to work for my room and board and went to school. Edward went to work on a farm for one dollar a day."

Mama took a big breath. "I learned English so well that I no longer remember much of my Danish. I wanted to become a good American citizen. I finally earned a teacher's certificate, which I knew would have pleased my father."

Mama smiled. "Then I met your father, a good-looking, black-haired young man. I was teaching in a country school where a Lutheran clergyman came every two weeks to preach. His son Philip, who always drove with him, had been away attending normal school in Galena, Illinois. I guess he fell in love with me. Anyway, he asked me to marry him and I did. I wanted a home of my own."

Remembering about the nobleman in Denmark, Carolyn said, "Did you love Papa?"

Mama was silent so long that Carolyn thought she had not heard her. Finally she said, "I grew to love him. And I respected him. He was from a good, hard-working, religious family."

Her eyes became dreamy. "We've been happy. We have you three loving children. That is more important than anything else. It's been a good marriage."

Carolyn was not sure that respect was the way a marriage should start. She liked the idea of romantic love, but it *had* been a good marriage. Papa and Mama never fought, they respected each other's wishes, and they were good and loving parents. Not like one family they had known once who fought all the time and whose children were always hungry.

Perhaps respect was a good way to start, after all.

"Mama, how did we all happen to come west in covered wagons? It must have been hard on you and Grandma. About all I can remember of that trip was sometimes a shortage of water and how thirsty we would get. Didn't we have a good home in Iowa? Both you and Papa were teaching school, weren't you?"

Mama smiled. "Yes, we had a good home but it was Grandpa's, not ours. We wanted our own home. When Papa learned that the United States government was giving free land to pioneers who homesteaded in Washington Territory, he wanted to get out here and get some of this free land. I don't think any of us realized it would be such a hard trip in our four wagons with all our worldly goods.

"In the two years it took us, the men worked from time to time in many places—on the newly built railroad coming west, in lumber camps—any kind of honest work they could find. It's been worth it. We have our own place now."

She did not mention that the first year here also had been hard. With their money almost gone, it had been difficult getting started when so many things were needed, like milk cows, horses for working the land, chickens for eggs, sheep for wool, machinery, and so on.

"Mama." Carolyn looked at her mother standing so tall and straight and pretty, still clutching the Spokane paper about the man Ditlef Carsten wanting to see them. "Mama, have you ever been sorry you came to America?"

"Never!" Mama's chin lifted high. "It is a very different life from what we had in Denmark. But if one loves God and tries to live a godly life, any country is a good place to be. I do wonder now what is going to happen. Why is Ditlef Carsten trying to find us? I'll admit that I didn't expect the past of so long ago to catch up with us here."

Carolyn was wondering about the poison ring. Now did not seem to be the right time, but someday she knew Mama would show it to them.

FIVE

A DROPPED
LETTER

It was only two weeks until Christmas and more and more corn was being popped and strung on the long strands of waxed thread. Carolyn and Frances were also making sugar cookies with the tin cookie cutters that Mama had brought with her. These included a Christmas tree, an angel, a horse, a cow, and a Santa Claus. The cookies were being pierced with small holes, then frosted to hang on a Christmas tree. A few gingerbread cookies were also made.

The children were not yet sure about having a Christmas tree, but Mama insisted they get everything ready to trim a tree just in case Santa did bring one. Carolyn was sure he would, but she did not let Little Sister know how she felt.

Mama herself was making candles, using beeswax and tallow. The beeswax came from the honeycomb in a big hollow tree the men found down in the Coulee during the fall. The tallow came from butchering one of the steers and a hog just as the weather turned cold but before it started snowing.

Mama often spent long periods of time in her and Papa's bedroom, with the door closed. Carolyn guessed she was making things for Christmas, knitting perhaps, but when she came out she did not say anything. She went about her usual business. Sometimes she pulled string from her big string ball to make wicks in the two iron candlemakers she had brought from Iowa.

When Carolyn was not making cookies she was making a nativity scene with the baby Jesus in a small manger of sticks and weeds. Her little ceramic sheep was just right as one of the animals. She drew a picture of a cow and a small donkey on cardboard and placed them near the sheep. Shepherds stood nearby with their long crooks for herding the sheep.

All this time Frances was practicing her cradle song about the baby Jesus. She had been trying to pedal the organ and play and sing at the same time, but soon she gave up. Finally she went over to Carolyn who was working at the long table.

"I can't play the organ and sing," she said. "My legs aren't long enough to keep the pedals going. Will you or Mama play for me, please?"

Carolyn continued with her nativity scene. "Please," said Frances. "I can't tell if I'm getting the tune right unless I can sing with the music."

"Let me finish this, honey, then I'll help." But

before Carolyn could finish, Eddie came in from the barn. He spoke to her and his voice sounded urgent.

"Sis, how'd you like to come with me to find Spots?" Spots was the pinto pony that Louie had given him after they found the wild stallion, White Cloud, the first summer they were there. Carolyn knew how much the pony meant to Eddie.

"I think the weather is getting worse and I don't want to lose Spots. He should have come in by himself. He may be hurt or something."

Carolyn knew that the "something" could be that an animal, perhaps a mountain lion, had killed him. Those mountain lions were vicious animals, especially when hungry. One had killed the mother of Carolyn's pony, Flame, two years earlier.

"What can I do?" asked Carolyn. "If you're skiing you can go faster alone. I'll just hold you back."

"Yes, but if something is wrong, one of us can go for help and one can stay with Spots. I brought in the extra skis I made for you."

Eddie was getting good at making skis out of barrel staves, and Carolyn liked to ski. She had not skied yet this winter.

Thinking of the stranger on snowshoes, she said, "Is the snow soft? Wouldn't snowshoes be better?"

"Maybe," said Eddie shortly, "but we don't have snowshoes and we do have skis. Coming?"

Carolyn looked over at Frances. "Oh, dear, I promised Little Sister I'd help her with her song for the entertainment. I. . . ."

Mama, sewing at the other end of the big kitchen

table, said, "You go ahead with Eddie and I'll help her." As she started to get up, she dropped her thimble.

Frances had been watching the older children but now she dropped to her knees to find the thimble. It was a small silver one that came from Denmark. Mama had had it for a long time and all the children knew she would hate to lose it.

Now Frances, crawling under the table on her hands and knees, found the thimble all right, but she also found something else—a letter which must have dropped when the mail was sorted. No one had missed it.

She crawled out, the thimble in one hand and the letter in the other. She handed both to Mama, who said, "How could this have been under the table all this time?" She held up the letter, then looked at Carolyn. "Don't you sweep under there?"

"Sometimes I don't sweep very well," admitted Carolyn, "if I'm in a hurry."

Mama did not say anything more. This made the girl uncomfortable because she knew she had been careless. Mama did not like anyone around her to be negligent about anything.

Carolyn was surprised at Mama's reaction to the letter. She sat staring at it without moving.

Papa, who'd come out of the bedroom just before Frances found the letter, also noticed Mama's behavior. "Louisa, are you all right?"

"I—I'm all right," she said slowly, "but I wonder

why *now* a letter comes from Denmark. From Copenhagen."

Carolyn had never seen her mother so hesitant, as though she were afraid to open the letter.

"We didn't know anyone in Copenhagen. That's the capital of Denmark and we lived way up north from there." She turned over the envelope again. "I don't remember that we had relatives there. It's been so long."

Papa reached over and took the letter out of Mama's hand. He read the return address and smiled. "Well, it can't be all bad. It's from the Dansk Genealogisk Institut in Copenhagen, Denmark. I suppose that's the same as our genealogy societies here. Maybe someone left you some money." He smiled at his little joke as he handed the letter back. Mama continued to stare at it.

"What's genealogy?" asked Carolyn.

"It's the study of family pedigree or history," said Papa. "People in America aren't doing much of that yet but they will someday. Many people in Europe can trace their history back into the early centuries. We're such a new country and people are so busy getting settled that there is no time for that now."

He looked at Mama. "Well, Louisa? Are you going to open the letter or shall I?"

Mama slowly picked up her scissors and carefully slit the long envelope. She was careful not to tear the return address or to damage the stamp. She pulled out one sheet of official-looking paper. She read it quickly and shook her head, then handed the letter to Papa. She looked into the envelope and pulled out another letter. She handed that one to Papa without reading it.

He finished reading the first letter, then quickly read the second one. He had been frowning but now he smiled.

"So it isn't a joke. You *have* been left some money, you and your mother. By that cousin you said stole your father's money. Or by his estate, rather. He's dead." He looked again at the letter. "It says, 'to anyone of the family who is alive.' This second letter is from a lawyer. The first one helped trace where you're living now."

"My mother!" exclaimed Mama. "Of course! We must show her this. We can't ask her to come over in this snow. Perhaps, Eddie, you can drop these off if you and Carolyn are going out."

"Sure," said Eddie. "Coming, Sis?"

Carolyn had not been out on skis for a long time. She felt she should stay right where she was, but she dearly loved to ski.

"Yes, I'm coming." She went upstairs to dress for the out-of-doors. This time she wore a pair of Eddie's old pants that were too small for him. She didn't like to wear a dress when out in the snow. Eddie must have really wanted her to go with him or he would not have been so insistent.

When Carolyn came downstairs, Mama handed her a sack of sandwiches. She had first wrapped them in some brown waxed paper and then put them into a small salt sack.

"You children may be out longer than you think. Fortunately, the bread is fresh from yesterday's baking and some of that leftover roast beef makes good filling for sandwiches. If you're late getting home, this will keep you from being so hungry."

"Goodness," said Carolyn, "we don't expect to be out that long. Or will we be?" She looked at Eddie.

"We shouldn't, but we'll take the sandwiches. In the snow and this time of year anything can happen."

Carolyn knew that her brother could eat any time.

So Eddie and Carolyn, bundled up against the cold, started on their skis toward Grandpa's cabin. It was still early in the day so they shouldn't have any trouble finding the pony after leaving Grandpa's.

Grandma was busy spinning some raw wool into yarn, but she got up from the spinning wheel to begin reading the letters.

She was slow in reading English so Eddie and Carolyn did not wait. Grandpa would also read the letters and he would help her to understand what they said.

Whatever their message, it must be important to come all the way from a lawyer in Denmark.

S I X

SNOWSTORM

As they left Grandpa's place, Carolyn looked up at the sky. "My goodness, it looks as though it might snow."

During the last few days the sun had been shining but now the sky was an overcast gray—dismal looking and cheerless. Carolyn did not really care. It was good to be swooshing along on skis again. The air was crisp but not too cold to enjoy its freshness. She took big breaths as she swung her arms and concentrated on staying in the trail that Eddie was making. Breaking trail was the hard part.

"Could be," said Eddie. "That's the reason I wanted to get out and look for Spots."

Carolyn was carrying the lunch in a little sack that Papa had fixed over her shoulders, while Eddie carried a larger sack partly full of oats for the pinto, if and when they found him.

Before long Carolyn thought she felt a difference in the feel of the air on her face. Was it getting colder?

She watched Eddie's back. He seemed to be skiing faster than when they started.

They finally came within sight of the high Coulee wall. Most places along the wall were straight down and the snow could not stick. Eddie turned and began following along the edge, continually glancing down. Maybe the pony *had* fallen over the rim. If that were the case, even Eddie's long rope with the hackamore on it could not help.

She saw coyote tracks crossing their trail and then some smaller tracks. The coyote was evidently chasing a jackrabbit.

Carolyn did not know how long they had been skiing when suddenly she noticed a long, thin spiral of smoke slowly rising from the very edge of the cliff. It was so thin it was hard to see at first.

Eddie turned suddenly and skied over to look down the side. Carolyn followed to stand beside him. Neither said anything at first. Then Eddie said, "Must be a cave down there with someone living in it."

"Maybe it's just someone lost who is camping there until the weather gets better." Carolyn turned to look at him.

"Maybe." Now Eddie stared all along the side of the Coulee wall. Finally he pointed to a snow-covered path coming up from below. It was not as steep as the wall.

"That must be where whoever it is comes up," he said. "Let's keep going. Over farther is a place where we might be able to go down."

"Can we go down on our skis?" Carolyn sounded doubtful. "How will we get up again? I don't think I can do that."

Eddie was thoughtful. "I guess we can examine the cave some other time. Right now I'd rather find Spots. Let's keep going along here. Over a little farther is a small pasture area where horses gather in the summer. Maybe we'll find Spots there."

They turned to the right and skied silently along the edge of the cliff. Neither child had been watching the weather although Carolyn was aware that it was getting darker.

"Say, I think you're right," said Eddie suddenly. "It *is* going to snow. Look!" He was pointing one mittened hand.

Out over the wide Coulee, toward Steamboat Rock, was what seemed to be fog. As they stared, Carolyn felt mist on her cheeks, so fine she did not realize it was snow—thin, tiny flakes that melted instantly on her face.

"Eddie!" she gasped. "We're going to get caught in a snowstorm."

"We'll be all right if it doesn't turn colder," he said calmly. "We can dig in and we won't freeze. There's no wind blowing."

Carolyn had to be satisfied with that, but she was feeling uneasy. Last winter a man had been caught out in a blizzard and had frozen to death. She certainly didn't want that to happen.

She noticed, however, that Eddie hurried their pace

as he kept looking. Since no wind was blowing, at least this was not blizzard conditions.

The farther they went the darker it became. Finally, Carolyn was sure they were lost and she refused to go another step.

Eddie said, "I *think* I know the way but it's really hard to be sure with all this snow. Maybe we'd better dig in and wait until morning before trying to find our way home. I'm hungry."

Carolyn had forgotten about the sandwiches. She said, "Why don't we eat a sandwich, then dig into a big snowdrift and stay until morning. Others do it."

A neighbor boy, when caught in a snowstorm winter before last, had simply dug in; when his folks found him the next day he was fine.

Eddie was sure that when daylight came they would be all right. Then he could get his bearings and find the way home.

Carolyn, on the other hand, feared they were lost for good. All she could do was hope that Eddie was right.

She took off one mitten and reached into the sack to take out a sandwich. She handed it to Eddie and suggested they had better save the other two until morning. Then she took out one for herself and discovered that never had anything tasted so good. Mama was smart to think of sending a meal with them.

They moved around as they ate so they would not get cold. Eddie stomped his feet and looked around.

"Look at that snow!" he exclaimed. "The flakes are getting bigger."

Yes, it was snowing harder. Carolyn had noticed and wondered what it would be like after a night of this.

As Eddie finished eating, he began to paw into one of the snowdrifts that was apparently banked against a big sagebrush. It was higher than most of the surroundings.

As Carolyn helped she said, "I wish we had a stick or something to dig with. Underneath it's hard."

"How about our skis?" Eddie stopped to undo his ski bindings. "We'll make a little cave for both of us to crawl into. That way we can keep warmer. I don't know how this will work but we shouldn't freeze, anyway."

Carolyn took her own skis off and they both dug hard. Soon they had a hole big enough to crawl into.

"Let's try it," said Eddie as though reading her thoughts. "I'm getting warm." He was puffing a little. "If we're warm when we crawl in, we should be able to stay warm all night. Better pull your stocking cap way down and wrap your scarf tighter around your neck."

"Eddie, do you have any idea what time it is?" Carolyn could tell time when the sun was out but not when it was dark.

"Not really," he grunted, crawling into the small cave to see how it fit for size. "Early evening, I guess." Then he backed out. "More digging," he added. Both began the work again.

The snow was now coming down harder. "I think we almost have it." Eddie again crawled in, then out. "If we lie with our backs to each other, we should be able to stay warm. Good thing you're wearing that pair of my old pants. Our heavy coats and socks Mama made are just right. And it's a good thing there's no wind." He grunted.

"Now try it. When you're in, push against the snow in the hole and pack it, then I'll get in. Here," he added, "let me have your skis. I'll stick them straight down through the snow so *if* anyone should come along, he can see the skis and know someone is underneath."

Carolyn did as he asked, then crawled in and curled herself into a tight ball, wrapping her arms around her knees to help keep in her body heat.

She felt Eddie crawl in and shove his back against hers. He must have curled in the same way after carefully shoving the feed bag in first. He would use that as a pillow.

"I wonder if Mama and Papa are worrying," she said softly. "You know how Mama always worries if we don't get home when we should."

"Of course they're worrying." His voice sounded muffled. Was he as worried as she was—or maybe he just had his mouth covered with his scarf?

Eddie continued, "They can't help but worry. But we'll be all right under the snow. At least we can't freeze."

Carolyn could feel him squirming deeper into the snowy hole. Now his voice was more muffled. "If only the snow stops by morning. If it does we can keep looking for Spots before we go home."

He did not say what would happen if it did not stop.

She had one more thing to say. "Eddie, did you know that Mama had been in love with another man besides Papa?"

"No, of course not!" His voice sounded rough. "But she loves Papa now. That's all that's important. Go to sleep."

Carolyn could not go to sleep immediately. She kept thinking of the letter and the man who stole the money and how it was going to affect their lives if some money was now paid back from his estate.

She did not think she would sleep but soon she dozed off. She awoke only once during the night. She felt stiff from her tightly rolled up position and stretched out as much as she could. Listening to Eddie's heavy breathing, she was surprised that she felt so warm. Soon she fell back asleep.

When she awoke again it was lighter, even under their heavy blanket of snow. She still had one arm wrapped around her upright ski. She felt stiff and cramped and when she tried to turn she could barely move. A heavy weight seemed to be pressing her down.

She felt Eddie move. Then he said, "Say, it must have snowed a lot. We have plenty on top of us."

She felt him squirming as he tried to kick the snow

out of the opening at their feet.

"Boy, am I ever hungry! How about that other sandwich?"

Carolyn felt around and found she had been sleeping almost on top of the little sack that Mama had put the sandwiches in.

"My goodness, I'm afraid I've squashed the two sandwiches left." She tried to open the sack but soon gave it up. It was too crowded. She would try again as soon as they got out of the hole.

Finally Eddie backed out and she could feel him jerking and pulling on the upright skis. Then she felt him digging the snow out at her feet. Soon she was able to back out of the hole and stand up.

The sun was shining brightly. They would have to wear their caps low and keep their eyes squinted to save their eyes from the glare.

Eddie was looking all around. Between where they stood and the Coulee wall was a dip in the bench land that would be an ideal place for horses to feed.

"Spots might be over that way," he said. "Let's ski toward that."

With the new soft snow, skiing was slow, but again Carolyn let Eddie lead the way. She was wondering if snowshoes might be better in such soft snow. While she was debating the merits of snowshoes over skis, she heard Eddie say, "There they are! And there's Spots!"

Carolyn looked up. Beyond them was a small herd of horses and a few cows trying to paw down through the snow to get to the bunchgrass buried beneath.

With the new snow on top, it made a long way for the animals to dig.

"If it turns really cold and the snow hardens, it'll be hard for the horses and cows to find enough to eat," said Eddie. "I'm going to catch Spots and take him home with us."

With that he started to speed up, then stopped suddenly and put his fingers to his lips. He gave a shrill whistle. "Why should we go over there when Spots can come to us?"

The pinto lifted his head and pricked up his ears.

Again Eddie whistled. This time they could hear the pony whinny. "Come on, boy," he called. "Come on!" Eddie continued to stand quietly.

"Will he come to us in all this snow?" Carolyn was squinting hard to keep the sun out of her eyes.

"I think so. At least, I hope so." Eddie nodded. "Remember he's been coming to me ever since I taught him to come when I whistled, right after Louie gave him to me. We'll see!" He lifted the feed bag high in the air. "Come on, boy!"

Spots did indeed come toward them, with two other horses following. One was King, the big bay gelding, and the other was the mare Nell, both family horses. Nell was the same reddish brown, but smaller than King.

It was slow going for them because the snow was almost chest high and it took strength to push against it.

As soon as the animals reached the children, Eddie gave each some of the oats in the feed sack. He slipped the hackamore over Spots' nose, then turned to Carolyn.

"Do you want to ride?"

She shook her head. "No, I'll ski. They'll have enough trouble getting through this mess without any extra weight. Say, are you going to check that smoke we saw coming up from that cave?"

Eddie shook his head. "Not today. We'll try to get to it when there isn't so much snow. I can't imagine why anyone would want to be living in a cave now."

Leading Spots, with Nell and King following, he turned and started toward home.

At least Carolyn hoped it was toward home. It seemed to her that Eddie was leading them off to one side, but since he acted as though he knew where he was going, she would follow. *She* certainly was not sure where they were. The snow made everything look different and it was very hard walking for the horses. Luckily, skiing wasn't bad.

The horses floundered along slowly, snorting and blowing out their breaths every few minutes. As they neared home, however, the snow was not so deep and it became easier going.

Finally they arrived. Carolyn could not believe it when she recognized their own big barn. Eddie put the horses inside to feed and water while Carolyn went on to the cabin to tell Mama they were home.

Mama was as glad to see her as she was to see Mama. It was good to have her arms around her mother again and to smell the soft fragrance that came from the little sacks of sachet, usually lavender, which Mama grew in their garden, dried, and then spread through her clean underclothes.

Eddie came in and Mama gave him a hug and a kiss and told him to wash and sit down at the table. She soon had bowls of thick beef stew set before them, then made cups of hot cocoa with rich cream and honey.

Carolyn could hardly wait for Eddie to ask the blessing before she began to eat. Never had anything tasted so good as that hot cocoa. God was indeed good to bring them home to such food.

After they were fed and warm, Carolyn felt terribly tired. She excused herself and went upstairs to her bed. She lay down, pulling a heavy quilt over her, clothes and all.

She was so tired that she forgot to ask Mama what Grandma had thought of the letter from Denmark.

SEVEN
THE POISON RING

After a good night's sleep, Carolyn forgot about their ordeal in the snow and thought again of the letter from Denmark. She asked Mama what Grandma thought of it.

"She's as surprised as I am." Mama smiled. "After twenty years in America it is a shock to have something like this come up."

At Carolyn's questioning look, Mama said, "Oh, I guess you don't know what I'm talking about. Herman, the man who took the money from my father and made him lose all his property before we came to America, is dead. It seems that Herman told Jens about it. Maybe his conscience bothered him; I don't know. I didn't know Jens very well, even though he was about my age, I think."

For a moment Mama looked as though her thoughts

were far away, then she said slowly, "It was Christian who gave me the poison ring. Jens is in America now trying to find us; something about the money and the ring."

Carolyn stared at her. "You mean you and Grandma are really going to have some money left to you?"

At first Carolyn thought that Mama did not hear her.

Finally she said, "That money belongs to us. I'm just sorry that my father is not here to know about it. Or perhaps he does know. I think everything happens for a purpose; there is a time for everything. Even the Bible says that."

Mama was quiet for a moment. She was obviously thinking of another time and place.

She took a deep breath. "I'm sure God let this happen for a reason, even though we do not know what that reason was. Losing that money was dreadful. It was hard on all of us at the time. I wonder if it made Herman happy. I doubt it. Ecclesiastes says that whoever loves money will not be satisfied with money, nor he who loves wealth with gain." Then she quoted, " 'He that loveth silver shall not be satisfied with silver; nor he that loveth abundance with increase; this is also vanity.' "

Mama was rubbing her hands slowly as she talked. "I have always felt as though the loss of that money killed my father. He was such an honorable man. For some reason the rest of the family was left to live and to face life's problems. Without God's help we never would have made it. My mother learned many passages from the Bible which helped her, so I learned them too."

Mama seemed to have forgotten that Carolyn was there.

Suddenly she bowed her head and said softly, "I bless the Lord who gives me counsel, in the night also my heart instructs me; because he is at my right hand, I shall not be moved."

She took another deep breath, raised her head, and stared at Carolyn as if she saw her for the first time.

"And now the time has come to repair that awful damage. It has taken a long time for the lawyers to find us because of second marriages and changes in names of Grandma and Grandpa and my name, of course."

Carolyn looked startled. "Changes of names? You mean our Grandma and Grandpa have had different names?"

"Not Grandpa, but my mother and I. It was probably the similarity in names that made it hard to trace us."

She was quiet so long that Carolyn began to wonder if she had forgotten what she was talking about. Now Mama looked at her.

"You know that Grandma's first name is Julie. After her husband, my father Johan, or John Stender, died in New York, she came to Iowa to join us where we children were living with her sister, my Aunt Margaret, and her family."

Carolyn nodded because she knew this.

Mama went on, "You see my maiden name and now my married name are similar; Louisa Stender and Louisa Standar. And when Grandma married Grandpa, her name changed to Standar, too."

She stopped and appeared to be thinking. Carolyn was trying to sort out in her own mind all this new information.

Mama went on slowly, "No, I'm not at all surprised that the attorneys in Copenhagen had a hard time finding us, with all those name changes and two such similar names." She chuckled softly. "Herman died five years ago and it has taken all this time for the family in Denmark to find where we moved to after leaving Iowa."

"My goodness," said Carolyn. "My goodness. . . ." She did not seem to be able to go on.

Mama threw her arms around the girl's shoulders. "Honey, all things work out if we only believe and pray to our God Almighty. I spent hours praying over this whole thing. So did my mother. It was such a tragedy for my father to have had his life end without knowing his property would someday be restored. But maybe he does know. Maybe the good God in his wisdom takes care of such things."

Her arms tightened and she kissed Carolyn on the cheek. "All things do work out for good to those who love the Lord."

Her voice, very soft, brought tears to Carolyn's eyes. She thought of all the years her other grandfather, her mother's own father, had been hurt. Her heart ached for the family.

Just then Frances, cheeks rosy and eyes sparkling, with bits of snow still clinging to her leggings, came into the house. She had been outside playing in the snow and Eddie had been pulling her on the new sled. "My hands are cold," she announced, jerking off her red mittens tied to a string put through the sleeves of her red coat. She grinned. "I tried to take Kitty for a ride but she jumped out of my arms."

"Where's Kitty now?" asked Carolyn, taking a small hand in hers. "My goodness, your hands *are* cold!" She did not wait to find out where Kitty was. "You'll have to get warmed up first, then we'll practice some more singing. You want to have that piece just right for the program, don't you? In two more days we go to the schoolhouse for the entertainment."

She helped take off Frances' heavy coat, her stocking cap, and leggings, hanging them up near the stove to dry.

Carolyn's mind was not really on playing the organ because she kept thinking of what Mama had told her. But she continued to play while Little Sister sang her cradle song about the baby Jesus.

"That's good," said Carolyn. "If you sing like that for the program I'm sure people are going to like it. Just remember we'll all be singing in our hearts with you."

After they were through Carolyn tried to work on her weed arrangements but that did not seem right. Then she helped Mama make cookies for the entertainment.

She did not see how Mama could work so calmly

when before long she would be getting a large sum of money. At least it *might* be a large sum.

"Mama," she stopped once to ask, "do you have any idea how much money you and Grandma will get?"

Mama shook her head. "No, I don't. It was a thousand dollars that was stolen, so I suppose it will be at least that much. *How* much really isn't important, although it *will* be nice to have a bit of extra money to send you and Eddie off to finish your educations so you can teach school. Teachers are needed so much in this country."

She stopped and looked thoughtful and was quiet for a long time. "What *is* important is that the wrong against my father has been righted. I'll always be most grateful for that!"

The next day would be the day for the Christmas entertainment. The snow was too deep to go in the wagon, so Papa and Grandpa and all the uncles had shoved sawhorses underneath the wagon bed and now were taking off the wheels and putting on sleigh runners. They needed the big wagon because not only the Standar families were going, but also the Hudsons.

Papa and Eddie then filled the wagon box with clean, fresh-smelling hay and put the big canvas over the hay. Carolyn discovered it was the same canvas that had covered it when they came west.

And now the big day had arrived. The air was cold but the sun was not shining and everything was gray.

Papa, all bundled up, looked at the sky and said,

"I hope it doesn't snow before we get back."

Carolyn, dressed in her heavy brown coat and cap and mittens, had gone out to the wagon with him to put in the hot rocks and sadirons and heavy, homemade quilts with their bright stars and patchwork squares. They had been warmed by the stove to keep everyone comfortable on the three-mile drive to the schoolhouse.

"Tell Mama I'll pick up Grandma and Grandpa and the boys and the Hudsons, then I'll stop on the way back. You'll hear the sleigh bells when I return."

When Carolyn entered the cabin, Mama had just finished putting up her hair. She was wearing a bluish-orchid alpaca dress which looked lovely with her golden brown hair piled high on her head. She pinned her little watch to her bosom so it was easy to open to see the time.

As Carolyn watched, Mama reached into her special box and pulled out a large shell back-comb decorated with colored jewels. Carolyn caught her breath.

Mama was shiny-beautiful all dressed up like this! No wonder a nobleman in Denmark once wanted to marry her.

Now Mama did something unexpected. She poked one slender finger into the box, felt in one corner, and pulled out a tiny beaded purse. Opening the little purse she took out a big, elaborately carved gold ring, very different from the rings she was wearing.

The dainty ring she was wearing with her wedding band had a small opal surrounded by seed pearls in a delicate setting. She had told Carolyn that Papa had given her this ring when they were engaged. It had been his mother's. Mama treasured it and never wore it when she worked around the kitchen or did gardening in the summer. It was her go-to-a-party ring. Only they did not go to many parties.

She held up the big ring. "I can't wear this because it is a man's ring, much too big for me. It's the poison ring that Christian gave me so long ago as a remembrance ring. I'll explain all about it to you children sometime. See the hinged cover?"

With that, Mama lifted the tiny cover with her small fingernail which was almost the same size.

Carolyn stared and her mouth fell open. She started to say something, then she heard the sleigh bells. That meant that Papa was back and ready to pick them up.

Mama heard the bells also. She hastily put the big ring back into the small bag, then into the box, and closed the lid with a snap. "We'll talk about this when there's time to tell what the poison ring was used for."

Then she threw a dark blue scarf around her shoulders, put a small blue one over her hair, slipped on her heavy winter coat, and was at the door putting on her rubbers as Carolyn put on Little Sister's red stocking cap and buttoned up her coat.

Carolyn grabbed Frances' mittened hand and they all went out to the sleigh where greetings were happy and noisy.

Soon the poison ring was forgotten as everyone snuggled down warmly under either their own quilts or the warmed quilts that Papa and Carolyn had put into the big wagon box.

Now it was time for the long-awaited Christmas program.

EIGHT

A CHRISTMAS PROGRAM VISITOR

When the sleigh reached the schoolhouse, Papa stopped the horses. Carolyn saw that someone, probably the schoolmaster, had shoveled out a path to the schoolhouse steps. This made it easy to get into the building instead of wading through deep snow.

She threw off the quilt that covered her and felt the nippy cold around her. She crawled over the side of the sleigh, dropped down, and reached out her arms to help Frances. Two of the uncles were helping Mama and Grandma out, and Mr. Hudson was helping his wife. Another uncle then handed the bundled-up baby into Mrs. Hudson's outstretched arms.

Carolyn still thought of little Merrilee as a baby even though she was now a year old. Robert David walked along holding his father's hand as Carolyn took the hands of Sally Mae on one side and Frances on the other.

Papa drove on, with the horses slowly pushing through the deep snow, on around to the side of the building where he would tie them. Carolyn knew that he would then throw the heavy horse blankets over the animals to help them keep comfortable while waiting.

As the family went into the one-room schoolhouse, Carolyn noted that they were among the first arrivals. The air, fragrant with fresh fir, was warmed by a potbellied stove in the center of the room.

"Oh!" Frances was looking all around. "Sally Mae, look at the tree!" Carolyn glanced down to see the eyes of both little girls bright with excitement.

A Christmas tree stood where the teacher's desk, now shoved to one side, usually stood. On the very top was a glittering star, cut from a piece of shiny tin, which made the tree reach the ceiling. Strings of popcorn and colored paper chains were draped around and around the tree. The very end of each branch was drooping low with small, colored mosquito netting bags of goodies.

Candles had been placed everywhere, some on the windowsills and some on the teacher's desk. They were not yet lit but probably would be before the program was over.

More and more people were coming in. Some were nearby neighbors, some from a long way off. The settlers did not get together often, but when they did, they enjoyed visiting and swapping stories.

Heavy coats were being shed as the stove gave out its pleasant warmth. At first they were hung on the big strong nails pounded into the wall. When those were filled, coats were piled on the floor.

A woman with a small bundle in her arms walked over to one corner of the room and carefully placed it on the growing pile of quilts and heavy coats. She then turned back one corner of her little bundle. Carolyn saw that it was a baby. More such infants would be placed in that corner before the afternoon was over.

Carolyn felt a small tug at her sleeve and looked down.

Frances was still staring at the tree in all its shining glory, but now she looked up. "Is Santa Claus coming here?"

Sally Mae peeked around Carolyn's long skirt. "Does Santa come in the middle of the day? I thought he came only at night."

"I think he can come any time," said Frances. "Don't you, Sister?" Again she looked up.

Carolyn smiled. "I don't know." Then, not wanting to be drawn into this difference of opinion, she turned to Mama to say something, but Mama was talking to one of the women.

As more and more people came in, gradually filling the seats, some were having trouble getting their knees under the smaller desks. Soon the room was filled with people; the mothers and fathers and many children.

Mr. Gilman, the schoolmaster, a rather heavy-set

young man with wavy sandy-colored hair, finally stood before them, waiting for the room to become quiet.

He smiled pleasantly as he greeted them. "Merry Christmas to all of you. I am glad so many could come. I know it isn't easy in this snow."

He looked over the now quiet room. "We are going to start the program with all of you singing. I have one or two songs to suggest, but if any of you have a favorite we can start with that."

" 'Jingle Bells'!" shouted a small boy.

Having just come in a sleigh, Carolyn was sure his song came from that. Everyone laughed and said, "Yes, 'Jingle Bells.' "

"Very well," said Mr. Gilman, going to the organ. To the surprise of many, he sat down and began pumping, keeping his feet moving fast on the pedals as his fingers played through the beginning. Carolyn wondered how he could play so well without music. She could not play like that.

He stopped, held up one hand, then began to sing in a surprisingly clear tenor. Now everyone was singing and the little room rang with the jolly sound of "Jingle Bells."

When that song was finished, he turned the stool to face the people. "One more song by a mother or father, then I'll suggest one."

Quickly Mama spoke up. " 'Joy to the World.' "

"Yes! 'Joy to the World'!" cried other adults.

"Very well," Mr. Gilman said again, and again his strong tenor started the song, with everyone following:

Joy to the world! The Lord is come;
Let earth receive her King;
Let every heart prepare Him room,
And heaven and nature sing,
And heaven and nature sing,
And heaven, and heaven and nature sing.

After they finished singing two more verses, Mr. Gilman turned to the crowded room once more.

"Now I'll suggest one. Do you know, 'O Come, All Ye Faithful'?"

"That's good! Yes, that's good!" The people seemed to like everything suggested.

So once more he began playing and singing:

O come, all ye faithful, joyful and triumphant,
O come ye, O come ye to Bethlehem.
Come and behold Him, born the King of angels!
O come, let us adore Him,
O come, let us adore Him,
O come, let us adore Him,
Christ the Lord!

Two more verses finished, Mr. Gilman swung around on the stool and stood up.

"Now we're all warmed up. We can go on with our program. We are going to start with a skit by some of the older children. You know who you are. Will you come to the front, please?"

Carolyn was glad she did not have to go to the front for that. She had been asked to·be in that little play, but this sort of thing bored her. She felt that she was boring others when she tried acting. It just was not for her.

She began to wonder when Frances would sing her little song. She hoped it would not be too late because that would mean Little Sister might be getting tired.

As each child finished whatever he or she was doing, everyone clapped. Some were good and some not so good, but the teacher had seen to it that each child contributed in some way.

Finally, it was Frances' turn. Carolyn felt a bit nervous to be playing before so many people, especially after the way Mr. Gilman played, but she had promised Little Sister she would.

Now she picked up the music book from her lap, took Little Sister's hand, and they walked together to the organ.

Before Carolyn could begin playing, the little girl cleared her throat and said firmly, "I can play this song but the pedals are hard for me to reach so I asked my sister to play for me."

The audience responded with chuckles and then Carolyn played a short beginning. When she began again, Frances' clear, sweet voice followed the music perfectly. She did not look at any music.

> *Away in a manger, no crib for a bed,*
> *The little Lord Jesus laid down His sweet head.*
> *The stars in the heavens looked down where He lay,*
> *The little Lord Jesus asleep in the hay.*

She turned and smiled at Carolyn, then turned back and sang the second and third verses with just as much warmth and feeling.

As the song ended Frances bowed gravely, and the entire room broke into clapping. Some feet stamped the floor. Frances looked startled. She almost ran to Mama where she was helped into her seat and Mama held an arm around her.

Carolyn heard her say, "Why are people making so much noise?" They continued to clap, saying, "More! More!"

But that was all. Frances refused to go to the front of the room again. The word "encore" meant nothing to her.

She said to Mama, "If they are going to act like this, I'm never going to sing again for a Christmas party." She buried her face in Mama's lap, and nothing Mama could say would make her look up.

Carolyn leaned over and said, "People are acting like this, honey, because they like your singing. They clapped for everyone, remember, only they clapped a little louder for you."

Frances would not listen. She simply did not like all the "noise."

Now Mr. Gilman began taking down the little bags from the tree.

"Will each child come to the front, please? Santa has left something for each of you."

Some of the children were hesitant and held back, some marched right up. Only after almost all had been given their little colored bags did Frances peek to see what was happening.

Carolyn was trying to decide whether she should go up to get one for her little sister, when one of the small boys thrust a bag into Frances' hands, saying, "Here, this's for you. Mr. Gilman said to give it to you." Then he added softly, "I liked your singing."

Little Sister lifted her head enough to take the bag and barely said, "Thank you," then ducked down again as he said the last. It was one of the young sons of some new neighbors who dropped by when they were in the neighborhood. Little Sister once told Carolyn that she liked him.

Carolyn glanced at Mama and saw her lips twitch. Did she think that Little Sister was having her first admirer? Now all she said was, "Aren't you going to open your bag?"

Little Sister clutched it tighter as Carolyn tried to help her. Mama said, "Leave her alone. She'll get over it."

Carolyn began watching other children. Some did not know what to do with the small bags, and parents were helping them. When the bags were finally opened, the children discovered that they held hard candies. Candy was something they did not have often, unless they made it. So store-bought candy was a *real* treat.

Now the neighbors began visiting. The candles had been lighted as early twilight set in. Some, who had long distances to go, had already left.

Carolyn was looking toward Eddie and some of the older boys, wondering if she dare talk to them, when suddenly she was aware that someone was standing at her side.

She looked up into serious brown eyes that began to twinkle as she stared at him. It was a man, not young and not old, who said, "Is your name Standar?"

She turned quickly, only to discover that Mama was talking to a neighbor, and Papa was across the room conversing with some men. Grandma and Grandpa were sitting quietly just watching everyone. Little Sister had left Mama's side and was now talking with a girl about her own age. They seemed to be comparing what was in their small bags.

Carolyn turned back to the man. "Yes," she said slowly. "It is. That's my mother, and my father is over there."

"My name is Jens Hamilton. Does the name 'Jens' mean anything to you?"

Carolyn's eyes opened wide. That was the name of Christian Hamilton's younger brother! Could it be that this man was actually from Denmark? He did seem to talk kind of funny. She had better tell Mama.

"Excuse me, please," she said quickly and got to her feet. Mama had moved away from her as she had been watching the boys. She walked the few steps to touch Mama's arm. "Not now, dear," she said.

Carolyn did not know what to do, but this was something Mama had to know. "Excuse me, Mama. This is important. It's about Jens."

Mama started to say something to the neighbor woman. Now she turned quickly. "Did you say 'Jens'?" She glanced toward the man.

Carolyn nodded vigorously. Mama turned to the neighbor and said, "Excuse me, please. I have some important business to attend to." Then she followed Carolyn back to the stranger.

"I'm Mrs. Standar." She held out a hand. "You can't be Jens after all these years!"

"Yes, I'm Jens." He was smiling. Carolyn thought he was holding Mama's hand longer than necessary. Suddenly he bent his head and kissed the back of her hand. When he looked up he said, "Now I understand why my brother Christian wanted to marry you."

Hastily she removed her hand and turned to Carolyn. "Sister, go get Papa. I think we had better have a conference about this."

Mama didn't say "please." That meant she was flustered even though she did not show it.

Carolyn could think of only one thing. *He kissed her hand. He kissed her hand!*

She hardly saw Papa at first, then she had a hard time getting him away from the men with whom he was talking.

Finally, when she made him understand why Mama wanted him, he came willingly and shook hands heartily with Jens Hamilton. Carolyn wondered if he would be shaking hands if he had known that Jens had just kissed Mama's hand. Men did not kiss women's hands in this part of the country.

Mama was saying, "Do you live in Copenhagen? You speak English very well."

"I live in Copenhagen now, but we used to live farther north of there. I have been studying languages and I began to learn English when I knew I would be coming to America someday. This gives me a chance to learn something about your Indians and cowboys."

"Hmmm," said Papa softly. "Cowboys are no different from anyone else." No one paid any attention to him.

Mama said, "I have been over here so long I think I have forgotten most of my Danish. Let's go over to my mother. Maybe she can talk to you in Danish. She speaks it once in awhile when she has a chance."

When Mama explained who the man was, Carolyn was astonished to hear Grandma say something in her old language, and hear Jens respond. Soon they were chatting away like old friends, although sometimes Grandma had to stop and think what to say in her native tongue.

Mama listened for a moment and smiled. She looked at Carolyn. "I can understand some of what they are saying, but I've made no effort to keep up the language. I'm an American now."

Papa said, "I think we had better go home before it gets too late. I'll gather up the boys and we'll get the sleigh in front."

Carolyn wondered what Jens Hamilton would think when he found he would soon meet four very real cowboys.

Mr. and Mrs. Hudson, with their three children, were now standing near Mama. Robert David and Sally Mae were sucking on some of their hard candy. "Are we leaving soon?" asked Mrs. Hudson.

Mama nodded. "Philip has gone to get the sleigh. I want you and your husband to meet someone from Denmark. My mother and I came from there when I was a young girl. Relatives have been trying to find us for a long time."

"Denmark?" Mr. Hudson sounded interested. "That's across the Atlantic Ocean, isn't it?"

"Yes," said Mama, "we came over in a sailing ship in 1865."

Now she turned back to Jens and Grandma, who were still talking in Danish. She reached out and touched Grandma on the arm.

"Excuse me, but will you let Jens stop talking for a minute? Perhaps he will come home with us and you can talk more. Now I'd like to have him meet the Hudsons."

He excused himself from Grandma and turned. For a moment he seemed startled, then shook hands firmly with Mr. Hudson and bowed to Mrs. Hudson. Carolyn wondered if the color of their skin bothered him. She knew that it did some people. But he was so friendly and nice that she was sure neither Mr. Hudson nor Mrs. Hudson felt uncomfortable.

When Mama asked if he would come home and have supper with the family, he hesitated, then agreed to come, saying only that he would return to his own place afterward.

Carolyn wondered about the skis he put into the sleigh before he crawled in and sat down next to Uncle Adolph; but no one seemed to think to ask where he was living. If he had been using snowshoes she might think this was the man who had watched them that day of the first snow. He did not have a beard, though, so he could not be that person.

When he learned that not only Adolph, but also Will, Jake, and Louie were cowboys, he was indeed interested. Carolyn could hear the men talking even over the jingling of the sleigh bells.

The ride home was nice. The air was clear and the stars, small and frosty, were beginning to peep out of the dark sky. They seemed to prick the dark coldness and stillness.

As they left the schoolhouse, the sleigh bells jingling, Carolyn looked back and saw the light from the windows spilling out and running into the darkness. Mr. Gilman must be putting out the candles because they seemed to be going out one by one.

It had been a lovely afternoon and Little Sister had sung her song very well indeed.

Now they would have company for supper and maybe they would learn something more about Jens and Mama's past.

NINE

CHRISTMAS DAY

At last it was Christmas Eve. Carolyn felt that everything had been done to prepare for the following day.
Two geese had been plucked and the downy feathers
were drying, all fluffy and nice in flour sacks hanging
from the rafters upstairs. Mama had roasted one
goose with plenty of dressing. She had also made
four big mince pies to go with Grandma's spicy plum
pudding. Grandma would be roasting the other goose
tomorrow. And there would be plenty of vegetables
to go with the mashed potatoes.

The weather seemed to be turning colder. Carolyn
hoped it would not snow more because tomorrow
they would ride in the sleigh to Grandpa's place for
the Christmas sermon, have dinner with Grandma
and Grandpa, and then ride back home.

It had not snowed for sometime now, and it was
so cold that the snow already on the ground might

be crusted and hard for the horses to pull through. With more snow on top, it could be very rough going. They would be stopping to pick up the Hudsons. The uncles would ski to Grandpa's.

Carolyn wondered where Jens was. He had eaten supper with the family after the Christmas program at the schoolhouse; then he had put on his store-bought skis and skied into the night without telling anyone where he was going. Mama had tried to get him to stay overnight.

They had not heard from him since then, but neither Mama nor Grandma seemed to be worried about it. They just knew they would receive some money, probably after spring arrived and traveling was easier.

Mama said, "Wouldn't you children like to hang up your stockings at the fireplace?"

Frances looked at her. "You mean Santa Claus will put something in each one?"

Papa smiled. "All I know is that he said he was coming, so perhaps you had better be prepared. Putting up a stocking will be a start."

Without another word, Frances rushed upstairs to get a clean long black stocking and brought it down to hang on the fireplace mantel.

Now she looked at Carolyn. "Aren't you going to hang up one of yours?"

Carolyn smiled. "I think he just puts something in stockings for little girls."

Mama spoke up. "This time maybe both you and Eddie had better put up yours also. You can never tell, you know."

Carolyn and Eddie looked at each other. Long ago when they believed in Santa Claus, they had put up their stockings on Christmas Eve, but now they felt they were too old. However, since Mama suggested this, perhaps she had something in mind.

Smiling to herself, Carolyn went up to get a clean stocking for herself and a clean sock for Eddie. This would be a real surprise.

Finally it was time to go to bed, so all three children climbed the stairs to their beds. The upstairs was just an attic with a blanket hung between Eddie's cot and the double bed for the girls.

After heat from the fireplace and the cook stove had been rising all day through the open stairway, it was quite comfortable by bedtime. It was only on winter mornings that it could be bitter cold. Then the children would rush downstairs to dress.

Carolyn lay still a long time as she listened to the strange, subdued sounds below. There was muffled sawing and hammering and the spicy fragrance of fir. Papa must be putting up a Christmas tree. There was the soft rustling of paper, and suddenly Carolyn smelled the unmistakable perfume of apples.

What a heavenly smell! Papa must have bought some apples in Spokane. The first year the family had lived there, he had planted little Jonathan apple seedlings, but they were not yet big enough to bear fruit. In a few more years they would have their own apples.

All this gentle activity was accompanied by whispering and soft laughter. Mama loved to surprise people.

Little Sister, snuggled down at Carolyn's side, had gone to sleep long ago. Carolyn and Eddie whispered back and forth for a little while; but soon she could hear him breathing hard, so she knew he was asleep.

Then Carolyn herself dozed off and slept. It seemed to her she suddenly heard Papa singing and rattling stove lids. Morning had arrived.

She remembered unexpectedly that they had not said their bedtime prayers last night. She folded her hands and said a little prayer to herself.

"Thank you, dear Lord, for giving us a nice Christmas and for our wonderful father and mother and my brother and sister. In the name of Jesus. Amen."

She could hardly keep from leaping out of bed. Instead she called out "Merry Christmas" to the other children. Then they carried on a three-way conversation, waiting for word from below to tell them it was warm enough to go down.

"Did Santa Claus come last night?" asked Frances.

"I think so, but we'll have to wait until Papa tells us the room is warm enough."

Suddenly she called, "Papa! May we come down? It's cold up here. The nail heads are frosty." She had noticed them by reflection of the downstairs light when she first awoke. She could not remember seeing frost on them before.

"Soon," called Papa. "Soon. It's cold! The water pail froze."

So the children tried to be patient until he gave the word to come. Then they hopped out of bed, grabbed their clothes folded neatly and laid across the foot of the beds, and padded down the stairs. It was terribly cold on their bare feet but they did not even think of that.

Since the stairway was open, they were able to look into the downstairs room as soon as they cleared the upper floor. Papa had lit the small candles on the Christmas tree.

"Oh!" gasped Frances as she caught sight of the tree.

"Oh, Papa! Oh, Mama!" That was all Carolyn could say.

"Say, this's all right!" said Eddie. "Santa knew just what kind of tree to get."

"Merry Christmas!" said Mama and Papa together.

"Merry Christmas!" the children answered in unison.

The tree was beautiful, a perfectly formed fir tree that reached to the ceiling, with a tin angel on top. It was covered with strings of popcorn and colored paper rings and bits of tinsel that Mama kept very carefully from year to year. Now the tinsel sparkled from the lighted candles. The sugar cookies Carolyn had helped Mama bake were hanging from the graceful branches. She found out later that Louie had brought the tree from the Coulee. Dear Louie.

Eddie, still carrying his clothes tucked under one arm, walked over and looked closely at it.

"Say," he said again, "you did all right. Where did you—" He stopped suddenly and looked down at wide-eyed Frances. "I wonder where Santa found such a perfect tree."

Apparently Frances did not hear him because suddenly she became intent on the brightly colored packages underneath the tree.

Mama said, "You youngsters get dressed. We're going to eat first, then we'll open packages." Eddie had already slipped into the big bedroom to dress.

She turned toward the cupboard to prepare breakfast, then stopped to look at the children. "You may look into your stockings if you like."

Little Sister rushed over to her stocking hanging at the fireplace, her long white nighty barely covering her bare feet and her long hair loose over her shoulders. Carolyn had not yet had time to braid it.

Frances reached one slim hand into her long stocking and pulled out a yellow apple and then a shiny red one. Next she reached into the very toe and pulled out a tiny china doll and some hearts and stars of red and green candy. She kept saying, "Dear Santa! Dear Santa!"

Carolyn had already begun to dress near the warm fireplace. Under her long, loose nighty, she pulled on her undergarments. The heat felt good. She was glad they had waited until it was so nice and warm before coming down. She glanced at the big Seth Thomas clock on the mantel. It was only half-past six.

Carolyn glanced at her stocking and wondered about the bulge in the top. The smooth round bulge lower down would be an apple. Quickly she finished dressing, then reached over and slowly pulled out what was stretching her stocking so tightly. She caught her breath.

It was a fairy candle lamp with a dome cover resting on a saucer-shaped pewter base. As it came out further, she saw that the cover was satin glass, a lovely art glass like one of Mama's cherished lamps that had broken on the trip from Iowa.

"Oh, Mama! Oh, Papa! How did you know I wanted this?" Her voice was breathless. "My very own light to carry up to bed. It's beautiful—"

Still holding the fairy lamp, she turned and rushed over, giving Mama a hug and a kiss, then Papa. "Thank you! Oh, thank you!"

"Santa Claus knows everything," announced Frances calmly. "Why are you thanking Mama and Papa? You should thank Santa."

"Well, you'll soon be thirteen," Papa told Carolyn. "I guess Santa felt you are old enough to have your own little light." His eyes were twinkling.

Carolyn knew that the secret was theirs as long as Little Sister believed in Santa Claus. "They can thank him for me," said Carolyn, "the next time they see him." This seemed to satisfy Little Sister.

From his sock Eddie pulled a long harmonica, which left room for only one apple in the foot of the sock. He stared at the mouth organ for a moment, then started to grin.

"How'd you guess what I wanted?" He took a big breath.

"Santa knows," said Little Sister again. "Santa knows!"

"Time for breakfast," said Mama. "Then we'll open the packages under the tree. Get washed, everyone."

▲97

Papa said grace, asking blessings on everyone and thanking God for their good health during this Christmas season.

Mama had cooked up a big kettle of yellow cornmeal mush, which had been simmering gently and was now ready.

"I can fix some eggs if you want them," she said, "but with all the excitement I thought perhaps this would be enough."

"More than enough," said Papa. "Very filling."

He passed the honey to Carolyn. She put a big spoonful in the middle of her bowl of yellow mush and watched it spread out slowly. The thick cream that followed made it a dish fit for a king, as Grandma was always saying. Little Sister was too excited to eat all of hers.

As soon as breakfast was over, the rest of the gifts were opened, with more surprises to come.

TEN
THE BLIZZARD

The family never had such a Christmas! On his last trip to Spokane, Papa had found a new shipment of lamps of all kinds in the General Mercantile Store. Mama said he went wild. But Carolyn noticed that tears came to her eyes as she opened her gift of the colorful Victorian lamp now sitting in the center of the long kitchen table. Papa thought it a bit gaudy for a kitchen, but Mama said that is where everyone worked or studied, so they needed plenty of light.

The floral decorations on the rounded glass shade and the bowl for coal oil, all fitting into the fancy brass base, delighted her.

Then Mama watched Papa open her gift. "My gift to you doesn't seem much compared to that beautiful lamp," she said.

He opened it and held it up. "A heavy black muffler

to help me keep my neck warm during the cold weather." He kissed her. "Anything you make is just right for me. A man is lucky to have a good wife like you."

Now Carolyn knew why Mama had spent so much time in her bedroom. She had been knitting Christmas gifts.

Mama's gifts to the girls and to Eddie were knitted caps, mufflers, and matching mittens. Carolyn's was a soft green, Frances' sky blue, and Eddie's light brown. These were for dress up.

"Oh," gasped Carolyn. "I almost forgot!" She rushed upstairs and soon came down with her little nativity scene. "This is for you and Papa. Merry Christmas!" She handed it to Mama. "To put on the mantel of the fireplace."

Mama looked pleased. "Thank you, dear. It'll look nice up there." Then she looked startled. "My goodness, there's still one more gift for all of you children. Guess where it is." She finished putting the nativity scene on one end of the mantel.

Suddenly Eddie reached his long arms way around to the back of the tree, where a long, slender something was hanging. It was rolled up with a narrow red ribbon. He pulled it off the limb and stood looking at it in his hand.

"Well, open it," said Carolyn, "or let me." She started to reach for it, but he quickly untied the ribbon and opened it himself. He opened wide a little magazine.

Little Sister had stood up and was watching.

"Oh, Mama!" gasped Carolyn, staring down at the

copy of the *Youth's Companion* for the last week in December. "I've been wanting that for a long time. Mr. Gilman showed us a copy one day at school. He said we could learn a lot from it." Eddie, nodding, agreed.

Mama was smiling at the surprised and pleased looks on the children's faces.

"I had Papa send in a subscription for it when he went into Spokane in October. It's something we can all read. Even Little Sister can enjoy the section for little people. I'm glad you're happy with it."

She glanced at the clock. "My goodness! It's almost nine o'clock. We'll have to hurry if we're going to pick up the Hudsons and get over to Grandpa's in time for his sermon and to help Grandma with the Christmas dinner. We'll take their gifts. Maybe we'll ask the Hudsons to return with us and stay overnight. It might help them to enter into the Christmas spirit."

Papa hastily bundled up and went out, with Eddie following, to hitch the team to the sleigh. Soon they were all on their merry way. They stopped to pick up the Hudson family. As they reached the grandparents' cabin, Carolyn saw that two other families had already arrived for the Christmas sermon. Until a church could be built, Grandpa preached from his own home.

"Merry Christmas!" shouted everyone as Mama walked in with two big mince pies. She went over and put them next to Grandma's big plum pudding garnished with bits of dried apples with the red skins left on. Carolyn was carrying another pie.

Eddie followed, carrying the big roasting pan with the goose already roasted. He put that on the back of the range to keep warm.

Grandma was hugging the smaller children. Now she came over and gave Carolyn a big hug and kiss, then reached for Eddie. He started to back away.

"No, you don't!" Her bright eyes were dancing. "You're going to have a Christmas kiss and hug." So he stooped over to let her have her own way. "You're never too big to hug."

"God bless everyone!" cried Grandpa. He had not put up a tree. He said that the fine Christmas tree at Philip's was enough to see. But the big room was bright with trimmings that Grandma had made. They hung around the room and on the windows, and there were fragrant fir branches everywhere.

As soon as gifts were piled in one corner and coats were taken off, Grandma asked everyone to be seated on three rows of long planks that Grandpa had laid on some large blocks of wood. The long seats were now covered with folded blankets.

Grandpa, dressed in his black cassock, open Bible in his left hand, stood patiently waiting for everyone to become quiet. Mothers were holding small children.

He began, "Oh, Father of lights, from whom cometh every good and perfect gift, have mercy upon us this bright Christmas Day, the birthday of our Lord and Savior, Jesus Christ. . . ."

Carolyn tried to keep her mind on what he was saying, but she kept wondering when they would get the money that had been stolen so long ago. What would Papa and Mama do with that money? She thought of many things they needed. And the poison ring? Surely, Mama would tell them all about it soon.

Suddenly she realized that Grandpa was ending his Christmas message. "Hear us all who are sitting before thee and help us to do thy will for the year to come. Have mercy upon us, for the sake of thy dear Son Jesus." He paused. "Now let us sing the Doxology."

Most of the people knew it and did not need a book. Carolyn was surprised that they had not sung a Christmas song, but since there was no organ at Grandpa's, often no songs were sung. Sometimes one of the neighbors brought his accordion for music, but today he was not in attendance.

Mama gave the pitch and soon everyone was singing a cappella. Singing without accompaniment was not always easy, as Carolyn well knew, but everyone knew the Doxology, so they had no problems.

Praise God from whom all blessings flow,
Praise Him all creatures here below,
Praise Him above ye Heavenly Host,
Praise Father, Son, and Holy Ghost. Amen.

Then Grandpa said, "Let us pray." Now all were bowing their heads and clasping hands and were saying the Lord's Prayer along with Grandpa.

After the people who came for the service were gone and the Standars, including the four uncles who skied over from their own cabin, had eaten all they wanted of the huge Christmas dinner, the gifts were passed out.

Grandma was delighted with her new ironstone teapot with the apple design on it. She had been wanting one for a long time. Grandpa's gift was a small whetstone for sharpening knives, since his old one was pretty well worn.

Mama had brought the Hudsons' gifts over. Carolyn knew she could not stand having them watch everyone receiving gifts without them receiving any. Mrs. Hudson's gift was a lamp almost like Mama's and she almost cried with happiness over it. Mr. Hudson received a big lantern to carry to the barn to do his chores. Mama had knitted little afghans for Sally Mae and Merrilee. And she gave a tiny doll like the one Frances had to Sally Mae.

Papa, who had been handing out the gifts, pretended that he could not find one for Robert David. But suddenly he pulled out a small, brightly wrapped package which he examined carefully before giving to the boy. "This must be yours," he said, smiling. "Surely Santa Claus would not have overlooked a fine little boy like you."

When Robert David opened it, his big bright eyes were shining. "Oh, I like this." He held out a small harmonica to show his father, then looked at Papa. "Thank you!"

"I'll show you how to play it when we get home," said Eddie. "Santa brought me one too. We can play together."

Adolph, Jake, and Will each received cans of Prince Albert smoking tobacco. Louie did not smoke, so he was happy with a big bag of unshelled peanuts. He always liked something he could eat.

Finally it was time to go home and Mama talked the Hudsons into going home with them for overnight. They would stop at their cabin on the way and get some things they needed. Good-byes were said; and again the sleigh was brought to the door and everyone piled in.

Carolyn had a warm feeling that it had been a lovely Christmas. She hated to see such a beautiful day end.

As the horses pulled them nearer home, she felt the wind was getting stronger and colder. She buried herself deeper under the quilts and snuggled close to the two little girls who had covered their heads.

After they reached home Mr. Hudson helped Papa unhitch and put the horses in the barn and feed them. Mama was busy putting a small log into the fireplace and getting the cabin warm when the men came in from the barn.

Mr. Hudson looked worried. "It seems to be getting awfully windy. Maybe we should not have come."

"This could let up by morning," Papa said.

"Of course you should have come," Mama added briskly as she finished lighting her new lamp. Papa had put coal oil in it before they had left for the Christmas dinner. "Isn't this wonderful?" She glanced at Mrs. Hudson who was watching. "First time I've lit it. It's almost like yours."

Mrs. Hudson was a slender woman, wearing her

black hair in a bun at the nape of her neck. Mr. Hudson, also tall and slim, stood watching beside her, and Carolyn thought what a nice-looking couple they made.

Mrs. Hudson was saying, "How can we ever thank you for the lovely things you've given us and the many things you have done for us?" She looked first at Mama and then at Papa. "You've been so kind to us in so many ways."

"What are neighbors for, if not to help friends and neighbors?" Mama turned toward the room the Hudsons would share for tonight. "God has been good to us. Life would not be worth living if we didn't help each other and share what we have. I'm going to move two or three things out of the room. I'm using it now mostly for a storeroom."

Papa was wrong about the wind. It did not stop by morning. Instead, it got worse. The next morning, by the time he and Eddie and Mr. Hudson went out to milk the cows and care for the animals, he knew they were in for a blizzard.

They had to use the rope which they had put up earlier between the house and the barn, for a guide. They couldn't even see the barn or any of the smaller buildings from the cabin.

Carolyn listened to the wind swishing around and over the cabin. She stood at one of the windows, a little girl on each side of her, trying to look out; but all they could see was white—a whirling, boiling, rushing, gray-white snow.

On the other side of the room the windows were plastered with snow. She could see no movement at all.

It seemed to be getting colder. The cabin did not feel very warm, even with a roaring fire in the fireplace and one in the cook stove.

Frances slipped a hand into Carolyn's, saying, "Why doesn't the snow stop so we can go out and play?"

The older girl shook her head. "I don't know, honey. I guess this is a blizzard and blizzards sometimes go on for days."

She reached up and tried to wipe the frost from the window, then ended up by using a fingernail to make a tree and a star. Yes, it was cold when the windows stayed frosty even with roaring fires.

Papa started to open the door to go out again, but closed it. "All you can see in this stuff is the nearest snowflake. It's a good thing you Hudsons stayed here."

Mr. Hudson, sitting nearby reading, looked up. "Fortunately we don't yet have animals to feed as you do."

Mrs. Hudson, sitting near him doing some mending for Mama, said, "Someday we will." Her voice was soft and her dark eyes twinkled, and Carolyn knew she was happy to be living in eastern Washington Territory.

For two days the blizzard raged, keeping everyone housebound. Snug in the cabin, Mama thought of all kinds of things for the children to do. At first she let the boys play checkers or dominoes. Eddie was good at both and showed Robert David how to play the games.

When they tired of that, she or Carolyn played the organ while the boys played their harmonicas. Even though Robert David still made mistakes, it did not matter. Mr. Hudson and Papa took turns playing the banjo with the singing.

Noticing that the children were growing restless, Mama finally pointed to the set of *McGuffey's Readers* on a short shelf that Papa had put up for her. Mama, as a former teacher, had brought her full set of *McGuffey's Eclectic Readers* with her from Iowa, insisting that her children study and learn new things wherever they were.

"I think it is time to do some studying. You can't play all the time," she said. "We may be in the wilderness but we don't need to neglect our studies just because no one can reach the schoolhouse during a storm. If we don't use our minds they waste away."

How often Carolyn had heard her say that!

Mama walked over and pulled from the shelf two slim volumes, a *Primer* and a *First Reader.* She looked down at Sally Mae and Frances.

"You two girls may use these." She handed the books to Carolyn. "Will you please help them?"

Carolyn herself was reading in a *Fifth Reader,* but she did like to help Little Sister. Now she had two little girls to help.

After the children all took turns reading, Carolyn

discovered that Robert David could read a little in the *Second Reader.* Since Eddie was studying hard to go to Courtland Academy for older children next year, he was reading now in the *Sixth Reader.*

Mrs. Hudson seemed continually amazed that the Standars were so willing to help all of them, especially their children. She said that in the South many people tried to keep black people from studying and learning to read. Both the Hudsons were happy to see their children picking up new words so fast.

Mama looked at Robert David. "Why don't you find a short verse to learn? Then later you may recite it for us."

Mr. Hudson looked up from a small book he had picked from the shelf, *Seekers After God* by Farrar, which he had been reading.

"I think that's a splendid idea," he said. "Good for memories."

Mama added, "Perhaps we can have a spelling bee sometime." She looked down at the children. "Would you like to have a spelling bee?"

"What's a spelling bee?" asked Robert David. "I never heard of a spelling bee." He looked at his parents.

Mrs. Hudson smiled. "I guess he's never heard the term. This is the way he learns."

Carolyn explained that it was a spelling match or contest. Perhaps they could have one sometime, but now they could learn some short verses.

Mama began reciting:

Monday's child is fair of face,
Tuesday's child is full of grace,
Wednesday's child is free from woe,
Thursday's child is delightful to know,
Friday's child is loving and caring,
Saturday's child is kind and sharing,
Sunday's child brings joy from the start.
Each child is special and dear to the heart!

Carolyn had heard Mama recite that many times. Now Carolyn said:

Wash on Monday, Iron on Tuesday,
Mend on Wednesday, Churn on Thursday,
Clean on Friday, Bake on Saturday,
Rest on Sunday.

Mama smiled. "Oh, you . . . ! Get on with you!" She looked at the rest of the children. "Now you see what you can do. We'll have a spelling bee some other time, but now you may learn some verses from the readers. Or perhaps from the Bible. You get the idea?"

ELEVEN
PASTIMES

The second day of the storm Mama suggested that the girls take the trimmings and cookies from the tree. Since they had helped make the cookies with tin cookie cutters in the forms of hearts, Santa Claus, and Christmas trees, they knew they were good to eat.

"That tree should come down before it gets too dry," said Papa. "We had better burn it."

"Oh, no!" exclaimed Carolyn. "Not yet."

"Well—," said Papa slowly. "Perhaps a few more days."

"Anyway, you girls wash your hands and take the cookies off so we can eat them," said Mama.

So Carolyn and the little girls washed their hands and started taking down the cookies. It was hard not to keep eating them, but each child was allowed only one cookie.

Eddie and Robert David were playing dominoes.

Mama and Mrs. Hudson were doing some baking while Mr. Hudson had been browsing through some of Papa's and Mama's books. He liked to read as much as they did.

Mr. Hudson said, "Listen to this from the Preface of *American Cottage Life* by Thomas C. Upham. 'It is the Bible, accompanied with prayer, which gives the American farmer his consistency of life, his strength of purpose, his strong and serene alliance with the truth, freedom, and humanity.' "

Papa nodded. "Yes, that book of poetry is a favorite of mine. It helped me to decide to come west and take up land. I needed that for my family to grow on. Homesteading is one way to get free land, but it hasn't been easy and sometimes I do wonder if I did the right thing. Teaching school, however, just didn't seem to be enough."

"You did the right thing," broke in Mama quickly. "You certainly did the right thing."

Papa looked at her and smiled. He did not say anything, but Carolyn knew he was happy with Mama's reply.

"I know," said Mr. Hudson, nodding. "I feel the same way. And it is good to know a family like yours. It makes our lives here much easier and more enjoyable."

Carolyn finished helping take down the tree trimmings, then she went over to the shelf of readers and picked two of them.

Mr. Hudson, watching her, said, "Do you want this space for your little class?"

Carolyn nodded. "Just this end of the table will do. I want to work with the children in learning some verses."

Most poems were too long so Carolyn decided to use only the first verses in some from the *Third Reader.*

"Little Sister, listen to this. Maybe you can learn it." She began to read:

> *Lend a hand to one another*
> *In this daily toil of life;*
> *When we meet a weaker brother*
> *Let us help him in the strife.*

"What's 'strife'?" Frances looked at the book. "And 'toil'?"

"Oh, my goodness, maybe that's too hard for you." Carolyn began turning pages.

"No, it isn't." Frances shook her head. "I know that 'lend a hand' is to help someone. It's just the other words I don't know."

Carolyn hesitated. " 'Toil' means hard work. And 'strife' means a struggle or fight to get along. Are you sure you want to learn this one?"

The little girl nodded, so Carolyn turned more pages, looking for something for Sally Mae. "Here's one. Sally Mae, listen."

> *Now the sun is sinking*
> *In the golden west,*
> *Birds and bees and children*
> *All have gone to rest.*

Sally Mae nodded. "I like that. I know all the words." She smiled happily.

Carolyn began looking for something for Robert David. "You should be able to learn one longer, maybe one of two short verses, don't you think?"

"Maybe," said Robert David cautiously.

"Listen to this," said Carolyn, beginning to read:

> *Tis a lesson you should heed, Try, try again.*
> *If at first you don't succeed, Try, try again.*
> *Then your courage should appear,*
> *For, if you will persevere,*
> *You will conquer, never fear; Try, try again.*

"What's 'persevere'?" asked Robert David.

"I know that's a hard word for you," said Carolyn, "but it's a good word to know. It means never give up in learning or doing something."

"I'll try to learn that poem." He nodded.

Carolyn smiled, then asked Eddie if he wanted her to pick something for him, but he said he would get his own. And it wouldn't be "The Village Blacksmith" by Longfellow either. He was learning a brand new poem. He flipped open a few pages and began to read:

> *The fisher who draws in his net too soon,*
> *Won't have any fish to sell;*
> *The child who shuts up his book too soon,*
> *Won't learn any lessons well.*

> *If you would have your learning stay,*
> *Be patient—and don't learn too fast!*
> *The man who travels a mile each day*
> *May get around the world at last.*

Mama must have been listening because now she said, "That's good! It can apply to you children or to us grown-ups."

Carolyn began looking for something for herself. She liked Longfellow's poems but most of them went on and on. She read "The Psalm of Life" with its nine verses and knew it was much too long, so she kept browsing. Finally she came back to the nine verses and decided to learn the first two and the last one. She read aloud:

> *Tell me not, in mournful numbers,*
> *Life is but an empty dream!*
> *For the soul is dead that slumbers,*
> *And things are not what they seem.*

> *Life is real! Life is earnest!*
> *And the grave is not its goal;*
> *Dust thou art, to dust returnest,*
> *Was not spoken of the soul. . . .*

> *Let us, then, be up and doing,*
> *With a heart for any fate;*
> *Still achieving, still pursuing,*
> *Learn to labor and to wait.*

Mama looked pleased and Papa remarked that he was happy his children liked to read and to learn such good sayings. This should help them all their lives.

The children began studying their poems, learning as much as they could now. Soon, however, the little girls became tired, so Carolyn put the books aside and said they could work on them later.

Mama said, "Maybe you'd like some exercise. I need water. How about bringing in some of that snow and we'll let it melt while the stove is hot. You should be able to get enough from the doorway. You can get pails from the lean-to."

Carolyn walked over and opened the door. She was astonished to see that the doorway was packed solid with snow.

"Papa! Mama! Everybody! Come look!"

Soon both families were staring at the hard-packed snow in the open doorway. Only it was not open anymore. It was just like another door, a white door without a doorknob.

There was simply no way out!

T W E L V E
LOSSES

"Well!" Papa scratched his head thoughtfully as he stared at the now solidly packed snow. "We seem to have a small problem. Certainly no one can walk through that!"

Carolyn stepped over to touch the wall of snow. Only it was not snow now—it was more like ice. She gave a push. No give at all.

Mr. Hudson had put down his book and now stood before the doorway also, staring with questioning eyes. He too touched the snow. "Say, that is really hard, isn't it?"

"Well, I never!" exclaimed Mama.

"My goodness!" Mrs. Hudson, with Merrilee at her side, said she had never seen anything like it. She grabbed the little girl as she started to toddle over to the doorway.

"Guess none of us have," said Papa.

Robert David was now leaning against it. He looked up at his father. "What happened? How are we going to get out? Don't, Sally Mae!" His sister was shoving against the snowy wall.

Their father shook his head. "The storm caused it. It blew the snow so hard against the building that it packed like this. There's just enough heat from the house to make the door slightly warm. The snow melted a tiny bit and froze. Now we have this." Again he pushed against the snow.

Without another word Papa turned and walked over to the small door going into the lean-to off the kitchen. He opened it, went in, and soon came out with two shovels and a tub he placed before the packed door.

Eddie, not saying anything, had been staring at the doorway.

Papa handed one shovel to Mr. Hudson. "Hope you don't mind digging. We'll begin this now to get enough snow for water. Tomorrow we can really start digging to make a tunnel to the barn. The blowing wind won't bother us down here."

"I certainly don't mind!" said Mr. Hudson. "Good exercise."

Papa turned to Eddie. "Son, get a couple of those pails out of the lean-to, will you, please? You and Carolyn can carry snow and dump it into this tub after we put it on the stove. We'll keep the tub full and have all the water we want."

Mama spoke up. "Better bring out the boiler too. You're probably going to have to take water out to the barn to water the animals."

"You're right, Louisa, as usual." Papa smiled at her. "Once we get this doorway cleared we'll dig the tunnel to the barn."

So Eddie brought out the big copper boiler and placed it on the floor beside the tub, and the men were ready to dig. Carolyn stood by with the broom to keep the snow from scattering out too far into the room.

Papa gave a shove with his shovel. Nothing happened! He did not make even a dent in the packed snow.

Without saying anything, Eddie quickly turned and went into the lean-to again. He came out with a hatchet.

"Good thing we didn't leave this one in the barn," he said, walking over and striking the icy snow. *Whack!* He soon had a section cut loose and the men began to dig, trying to keep all the snow in the tub.

That was impossible. Icy bits were flying everywhere. Mrs. Hudson put Merrilee into Mama's arms and she grabbed the broom next to the fireplace and began to help Carolyn sweep it toward the door.

Now Papa and Mr. Hudson were digging with all their might. They kept Eddie busy carrying the snow to the stove to dump into the boiler and the tub, as Carolyn and Mrs. Hudson kept sweeping toward the door opening.

The snow softened as the men dug out farther and soon they could almost stand up. Mama could not believe how much snow was packed before that door.

As the men were digging, suddenly part of the wall

to the tunnel caved in. Jake and Will slid down in front of the door. Their black mustaches and beards were covered with frost.

"Sorry," said Will, brushing off snow from his arms and body. "We left our skis and shovels up above. I see you have the same idea we had. The wind stopped blowing so we dug ourselves out from our cabin, checked on the old folks, and decided to come on over. Not much snow sifting down now but it's mighty cold."

"Ummm—," said Papa. "So the wind has stopped."

Mama looked at the men. "How in the world did you know where the cabin was? Isn't it covered with snow?"

Will grunted. "Yes, it's covered, but as we came along we saw smoke coming up from a big snowbank, then the very top of the chimney showed. Probably the heat from the fireplace kept it free. We figured it had to be the cabin. And here we are!"

Papa nodded. "The snow cover has been like a blanket over the whole house. We haven't felt the cold as much as we would've had we been out in the open. Anyway, you're more than welcome."

He looked at first Jake and then Will. "Did you say you brought your shovels?"

Jake nodded. "We left them up above with our skis."

"Good," said Papa. "I'd planned to dig a tunnel to the barn so we can take care of the animals. Their water must be frozen solid, and the cows need milking. With you here maybe we can get it finished today instead of tomorrow as I was planning."

"Let's go!" cried Will. They reached up for their shovels and both he and Jake began digging so fast it was hard for the children to keep the snow going to the stove to melt.

Robert David and Carolyn took turns carrying the pails of snow. As it melted Mama began dipping some out to put into kettles and pots and pans for their own house use. Mrs. Hudson helped.

It was not long before the tunnel was finished. The first thing Papa did, with Eddie's help, was to take a boiler of the hot water to the barn to dump into the big round wooden tub that had frozen over. This melted the ice enough so Papa could break it up for the animals to drink. Three more tubs of hot water mixed with the cold enabled all the livestock to satisfy themselves.

Carolyn followed the men out to see how things were with the animals. One of the ewes had been expecting and she hoped the animal was all right. Normally the animals were bred so that they had their babies in the spring when it was warmer, but somehow they had slipped up on old Rosie.

As the men began feeding the livestock and throwing feed to the chickens and geese, adding whole corn for the geese, Carolyn noticed the old ewe stretched out near one of the mangers. She walked over and looked down. Two tiny lambs were lying beside her.

Carolyn bent down to touch one lamb, then straightened up and called, "Papa! Papa! Come quick!"

As Papa came over to stand beside her, she said, "Look! Is Rosie all right? She's awfully quiet. Are the lambs all right?"

Papa gently touched the ewe, felt her heart, and picked up one of the lambs. He shook his head. "I'm afraid not. We didn't get out here in time. This lamb is dead."

"Oh, Papa, no!" cried Carolyn. "No!"

He now leaned over and opened one eyelid on the ewe. "Yes, she's gone too." He reached for the other lamb, which was lying tightly against the mother. "This one seems to be alive. Just barely. There's still enough body heat in the mother, that lying against her as this one did, saved its life. It's a little ewe lamb."

Carolyn felt like crying. "Why did Rosie die?"

"She's old. I'm afraid she had a hard time with the birth of these lambs, and the bitter cold was too much for her. Nature is cruel sometimes. If we could have been here a day sooner, perhaps we could have helped her."

He was wrapping the newborn lamb in a gunnysack. Now he handed it to Carolyn.

"Do you want to try to keep this one alive? It needs warmth and milk. We're going to milk the cows. They must be very uncomfortable with their hard udders. You take the lamb to the cabin and I'll bring in some of the warm milk right away."

So Carolyn took the lamb to the house, hugging

it close to her body. Everyone wanted to help when told what had happened.

"Poor little lambie," said Frances, stroking the tiny woolly white head.

"Poor lambie," added Sally Mae, not really knowing why it was a "poor lambie."

Mama immediately warmed an old piece of flannel cloth at the range and brought it over to Carolyn, who was still holding the baby animal.

"Take that gunnysack off," she said. "Here's a warm cloth to wrap around it. I'll get another cloth to heat and change off. We'll put an old quilt on the floor near the stove for it to lie on."

"Oh, Mama, thank you!"

As soon as Papa brought in the big pail of foaming milk, Carolyn poured some into a tin cup, then put a small piece of wadded cloth into it. She put it to the baby's lips and the lamb began to suck. As long as she held the wadded bit of cloth in the milk the lamb continued to suck noisily. The minute she took the wad away, the sucking stopped and the little nose began to bunt.

The big gray mother cat came over and sniffed. She was bigger than the lamb. Soon a pink tongue came out and she was licking the little animal. The lamb smelled the cat and gave her a little bunt. Kitty did not mind. She seemed to know this was only a baby without a mother. Both Mama and Mrs. Hudson stood watching.

Mama said, "I think you'll have to let the lamb suck the cloth for awhile. After it gets used to it, it'll learn to drink, just as calves learn to drink from a pail."

"I wish I had a nipple for it to use," said Carolyn, noting the long wagging tail as the lamb tried to get more of the milk.

"I agree with your mother," said Mrs. Hudson. "You know, if that cat had kittens now, she'd have milk. I'll bet she would feed it, although her nipples are rather small for a lamb, even one as tiny as this."

"It won't starve if you keep working with it," said Mama, going back to the stove to see how the melting snow was coming. She began to hum an old song they all liked, singing softly at times:

> *Be happy, no matter what evils betide,*
> *No matter on what your frail bark may ride;*
> *No matter how sullen the heavens appear,*
> *Be happy, for sometime the sky will grow clear.*

The big cat and the wee lamb became firm friends. The mother cat seemed to know that the newborn lamb needed help. After playing, they would lie down together, with the lamb's small nose snuggled against the warm body of the gray cat. Kitty would then throw one front leg across the lamb's slim little body. Now the animals were lying quietly sleeping.

Carolyn and Frances and Sally Mae were getting ready to go out to the barn as Eddie came in with a pan of potatoes, carrots, and dried onions. He and Papa had been digging snow away at one side of the cabin to reach the cellar doors. He said that with the frozen snow, it was hard to get the double doors open, then added that everything down there seemed to be fine. Nothing was frozen.

He turned to go out, saying, "Papa wants to know whether you want some fresh mutton chops or some of the frozen venison."

Mama turned. "Mutton chops? Why—oh!"

Matter of factly, Eddie said, "Jake skinned out the ewe that died. Since she was still warm, he says the meat is all right. He bled the body well."

Mama hesitated. "Oh, dear—I guess so. It just doesn't seem right to eat the mother of that poor little lamb. Yes, tell him we'll have the chops. Save the frozen venison for some other time. We can't let good food go to waste."

Carolyn, hearing this decision, was not at all sure she wanted to eat mutton now or later.

She looked down at Frances and Sally Mae. All she said was, "Let me help you button your coats before we go out to the barn. We'll play in the hayloft where I can push you on the swing and I'll swing on the long rope dangling from the rafters."

Mama, so used to the children playing in the big loft of the barn, did not even warn them to be careful. Only later did she realize the possible danger of playing in the barnloft.

THIRTEEN

A SCARE

The uncles, before returning to their cabin, offered to help the Hudsons get to their own cabin. Mama talked them out of it, telling the men to fix some barrel-stave skis for them first.

Robert David was helping Eddie work out a puzzle while Papa and Mr. Hudson were playing chess.

Carolyn was glad the tunnel was finished so they could get to the barn. The children loved going into the hayloft to use the swing that Papa had hung from the rafters. With strong pushing from Carolyn they could swing high.

The two little girls swung for a long time, then ran around jumping into the fragrant hay until they were tired. Finally they said they were ready to return to the cabin.

Before Carolyn could stop her, Frances darted toward the opening to climb down the narrow ladder nailed to the wall near the manger. Suddenly she stumbled and fell through the opening before Carolyn had a chance to grab her.

Carolyn screamed! She grabbed Sally Mae to keep her close to her. Staring down through the opening, the girls saw Frances stretched out on the barn floor below them. The little girl's body, her red winter coat opened wide around her, was dreadfully quiet.

Carolyn stood staring for a moment, then began to help Sally Mae down the ladder. Sally Mae's legs were so short it was hard for her to reach the rungs. Carolyn's full skirt caught on a splinter of wood but she jerked it free with her other hand as, with her body, she held Sally Mae tightly against the ladder.

"Dear Lord, don't let Little Sister be hurt bad," Carolyn prayed. "She's only a little girl. Please. . . ."

Then she and Sally Mae were on the floor kneeling beside the fallen child. Carolyn softly touched one pale cheek.

"Please, God, don't let her be hurt real bad."

Carolyn clasped her hands tightly, then pulled the little red coat carefully over the small body, so still and white.

She stood up suddenly, grabbed Sally Mae's hand, and started for the barn door. They would have to get help.

She opened the outer door and was hit by a blast of chilly air. The long snow tunnel to the house was still intact but it must have had a hole in it somewhere since the air was so cold.

The tunnel was not high enough for the men to

stand upright, but the two girls could stand easily.

"Follow me, Sally Mae. I'm going to run."

It was not dark because light from the sun, now shining brightly above, filtered through the top of the tunnel.

The girls leaped over a small pile of loose snow. Carolyn glanced up briefly to note a hole above her head where she could see a patch of blue sky. Sure enough, the overhead snow had fallen from a thin spot now open. Also, the big hole near the door was open, the hole in which the men had gone in and out.

She reached the door of the cabin and jerked it open. "Mama! Papa! Little Sister is hurt!"

Mama, her hair in ringlets around her flushed face, turned from the kitchen range where she had been stirring something bubbling in the big black kettle. She looked startled.

"What do you mean, hurt? How?"

Papa looked up from his game with Mr. Hudson. "Excuse me. I'll see what's happened."

He went to the wall back of the stove to pull on his heavy jacket and black cap that Grandma had made for him earlier that winter.

He and Carolyn quickly went out while Mrs. Hudson kept Sally Mae with her. She had been holding little Merrilee and now her arms were around both her little ones.

Carolyn followed Papa into the barn. He was just picking up Frances as Mama, now dressed in a heavy jacket and a scarf over her head, entered the barn. She rushed over to them.

"How did this happen?" Mama cried, pushing back the hair from Little Sister's forehead. "How could she have fallen through that hole?" She looked up at the ceiling.

"We were playing up in the hayloft." Carolyn looked uncertain. "I don't know *how* it happened, but she stumbled. I should have gone down first but she was too fast. I think she hit her head on the manger."

"Oh, no!" Mama clenched her hands together tightly and lifted her eyes. "Keep my baby safe, dear Lord."

"We'd better get her to the house where it's warm," said Papa gruffly, Frances still cradled in his strong arms. "She's awfully quiet."

Carolyn picked up a red mitten before she followed them out.

After reaching the cabin, Mama told Carolyn to wrap two sadirons that were on the back of the hot stove. She pulled out an old union suit from a flour sack of items she was intending to mend and handed it to Carolyn. "And put a big pan of salt on to heat," she added. "We'll put that in little sacks to help warm her."

Mama then rushed into the big bedroom to pull the little trundle bed out from under their bed so Papa could put Frances into it. Since Frances had been sleeping upstairs with Carolyn, the bed had not been used. A cot had been put up in the bedroom that the Hudsons were using, and Merrilee was sleeping in one end and Robert David in the other.

Mama helped in taking off the little red coat, then felt Little Sister's hands and forehead.

"My baby," Mama crooned softly, as Carolyn brought in the wrapped hot irons. "What has happened to my baby?" She took a small limp hand in hers. "Oh, Philip, she's so cold!"

"Yes, she's cold. We'll have to get her warmed up. Is that salt hot yet?"

"I'll see," said Carolyn, going out again. She returned soon with two small sacks filled with the hot salt.

Mama took them and put one under each arm. "Keep heating more," she said, "then we can put plenty of bags around her."

As Carolyn went out again, she glanced toward the fireplace. The big clock said it was almost noon.

The little body did not respond and Mama and Papa prayed together.

A day later, as Carolyn took her turn in watching the little girl, she saw the eyelids flutter. "Mama! Mama! Little Sister is trying to open her eyes."

By the time Mama reached the bed, the eyes were quiet but a few minutes later they opened again. Mama gave a big sigh.

"Thank you, Lord," she whispered. "Thank you for keeping my baby alive."

Mrs. Hudson, who had been helping all she could, gave a hearty "Amen" and "Thank you, Lord," and put one arm around Mama's shaking shoulders.

Mama wiped her eyes with a corner of her apron

and put one cheek against Mrs. Hudson's brown one, then moved away and straightened her shoulders.

"Thank you," she said. "It is such a comfort to have friends at a time like this."

"I know," said Mrs. Hudson softly. "I've lost two small children, and it was very hard."

She straightened her own shoulders. "I think we can get back to our own cabin now since the blizzard has stopped blowing in so much snow."

"Wait one more day," said Mama, as though she wanted another woman nearby. "The snow will pack in another day or two and will be easier to walk on. Maybe you'll have some skis by then because I'm sure either Philip or his brothers will fix you some out of barrel staves."

Mrs. Hudson was not sure she wanted to try to use skis of any kind, but she decided if that was the only way to get home, she would try.

FOURTEEN
MAMA'S SPECIAL BOX

The next day Frances was no better. While the grown-ups stood around the little girl, Carolyn was trying to keep the younger children quiet. Finally she took down *McGuffey's Readers* again and began to help the other children continue to learn their poems.

Then Robert David started tapping his teeth with his pencil as Sally Mae began teasing him by poking at him.

Carolyn stared at the children. She knew that Little Sister's accident was making everyone edgy and uneasy.

"Don't, Sally Mae, honey," she said softly. "Robert David is trying to learn his poem."

The little boy looked up at her. "I'm getting tired. Can't we go outside and play in the snow?"

Carolyn started to say something just as Mama

came into the room from the bedroom where she had been sitting with Frances.

Frances had moments of knowing her and the rest of the family, then she would go to sleep for a long time.

Now Mama held a small maple wooden box in her hand, a box almost a foot long, around eight inches wide, and four inches deep. She called it her "special box," and no one was allowed to get into it.

"Little Sister is sleeping right now and I wondered if you children would like to see what I have in this box."

She walked over and put it down carefully on the long kitchen table. Then she noticed that Eddie was gone. "Where's Eddie?"

"He said he was going to Grandpa's," said Carolyn. "Then he was going to check with the uncles to see if they have skis ready for the Hudsons to wear home."

Mama nodded. "Well, we'll have a few minutes to help pass the time with what's in this box. Would you children like to see my poison ring?"

Robert David exclaimed, "Poison ring? A real poison ring?"

Mama nodded. "That's right. A real poison ring."

At the other end of the table Papa and Mr. Hudson stopped playing their game of chess. Mrs. Hudson, holding Merrilee, came to stand beside Mama.

Now Papa said to Mr. Hudson, "You might enjoy looking at those things in that box, both you and Mrs. Hudson. They're rather interesting. My wife has had the box a long time. It came from Denmark with her when she was a girl. Then it came here from Iowa in the covered wagon."

Now Mama opened the box, carefully lifting the hinged lid. Inside was another hinged lid, a thin single layer of wood covered with a purple velvet cloth. The main box was divided in sections.

In one compartment were pretty colored buttons on a long string. Now Mama held them up.

"Many years ago when I was a small girl I began gathering buttons because I liked their color and the little figures on them. An aunt and an uncle traveled for the government while we still lived in Denmark. My aunt began bringing me buttons from all over the world."

She shook the string of buttons. "These came from Japan and are called Satsuma buttons because they were made from Satsuma pottery."

She carefully laid the string down and picked up a shorter string. "These buttons are hand painted on porcelain. Some of them are valuable, some are not. I've always liked them because of the lovely colors."

Carolyn reached over and carefully picked up a small colorful dish, smaller than a saucer.

"This little dish, Mama? Isn't it *cloisonné?*" She liked to roll the big word over her tongue.

Mama nodded. "Yes, dear, that is *cloisonné,* a very special kind of Japanese pottery. Each tiny flower leaf is outlined with a hair-like thread of copper wire."

She then picked up a colorful string of beads long

▲ 135

enough to go around her throat. "This is a multi-colored jade necklace that the same aunt brought me from China on another trip. Jade goes from white to dark green and is supposed to have spiritual as well as medicinal powers."

Noting that Sally Mae was getting restless at all the talk, Mama showed her the beautiful back-comb of tortoise shell.

"I wear this when I want to be very dressed up with my hair high on my head." She showed them how it held the loose back hairs neat and smooth.

"That's pretty," said Sally Mae, reaching for it. "I like it."

"Don't. . . ." Mrs. Hudson held out a hand, but Mama said she could not hurt it and handed it to her.

Then she showed them Papa's heavy Waltham watch and Mama's own little golden pin-on watch. Robert David wanted to hold the big watch so Mama put that into his hand.

Carolyn liked the bright pin-on watch. It always looked nice against Mama's shiny dark blue silk dress.

Mama said, "Now I'm going to show you my two cherished possessions."

She took from the box a long necklace of golden brown human hair braided with four strands instead of three, making it like a tiny round rope. Carolyn never tired of looking at it, and Mama never stopped warning her to be careful in handling it because it was very fragile and was beginning to come apart.

"This necklace was made of the hair from one of my great-aunts after she died," said Mama quietly.

"She had lovely long, honey-gold hair." Mama held it up. "Isn't this beautiful?" The hair was almost the same color as her own.

Carolyn was waiting for the bit of jewelry yet in the box, a heavy gold ring. She had only seen the ring once before, but she found it fascinating.

At last Mama reached into a corner compartment of the box and brought out a small knitted bluish purple string purse decorated with tiny silver beads.

Mama opened the wee purse carefully, saying, "This poison ring is special. It was given to me by a nobleman in Denmark who once asked me to marry him."

Mrs. Hudson caught her breath. "A poison ring! I've heard of them but I've never seen one before. I worked for a family in the South who was very proud of the fact that they owned a poison ring. It is something quite historical, I believe."

"Yes, I guess it is historical," said Mama. "Would you like to see this one?" She handed it to Mrs. Hudson.

"Oh!" Mrs. Hudson caught her breath again as she turned the ring over and over. "I heard them talk about theirs but of course I never had a chance to see it. I don't suppose it is poison now—is it?" She sounded doubtful.

"No," said Mama, smiling. "The poison was put into the little opening under the lid." She reached over and lifted the tiny hinged lid. "As you may know, these rings were used for. . . ."

At that moment a knock sounded on the door.

Mama looked startled and Papa got to his feet to go to the door. It was a different sound than when the grandparents or the uncles came. They usually knocked softly and then walked in.

Both Robert David and Sally Mae had stepped next to their mother to look at the unusual ring in her hand, but now everyone stood staring at the door. Sally Mae grabbed her mother's skirt.

Papa threw the door open and there stood a tall man bundled in a heavy brown fur coat. As the door opened he leaned his snowshoes against the side of the tunnel.

Carolyn gasped. He had a scraggly sandy-colored beard and as he turned, he looked just like the man who had been watching them when they were making snow angels. She must tell Papa, but how?

"Come in," said Papa, stepping to one side. "What can I do for you? You're a stranger here."

No! No! Don't let him in, Carolyn wanted to cry. *Don't let that man in!*

It was the policy of the household to be courteous to strangers, although Carolyn knew that if the men had not been in the house Mama would not have allowed the stranger in.

"I'm not sure whether I am lost or not," said the man, smiling slightly, "but. . . ."

He stopped talking as he stared at the table with all the jewelry spread out. Then his eyes opened wide as he stared at the heavy gold ring in Mrs. Hudson's hand. At first he seemed startled, then he took a big breath as though he wanted to say something.

Carolyn looked at Mama to see if she noticed the man's interest in the ring. She was amazed to see her mother frowning slightly as she stared at the stranger. Did she recognize him? Carolyn looked back at the man. She was sure that she herself had never seen him except that one time when he had been watching them.

Courtesy made Mama say, "Would you men like some coffee?"

She did not wait for an answer but went to the stove to make a fresh pot of boiled coffee. Since the stove and water were both hot it did not take long.

Papa hung the man's heavy coat on a peg near the door. The stranger could not seem to take his eyes from the jewelry on the table or the ring still in Mrs. Hudson's slim, brown hand.

Mama poured three cups of coffee and placed them on the end of the long table, along with a plate of fresh coffee cake she had made that morning.

Then she reached over and began putting all the buttons and beads and the big back-comb into the box with the compartments.

"We'll have more time for this later," she said. "I'll explain about the poison ring some other time. It's an interesting story."

Mrs. Hudson reached down and picked up the small purse, slipped the ring inside, and gave it to Mama.

Usually Mama put that ring way back in one corner of her special box, but this time she laid it on top of everything else. Little Sister had begun to cry and that, and the obvious question as to who this man was, left her a bit flustered.

Now she left the room, taking the box with her as she went into the bedroom to care for the crying child.

FIFTEEN
THE POISON RING DISAPPEARS

Papa finished drinking his coffee, excused himself, and followed Mama into the bedroom. Carolyn knew that he was as worried as Mama about Little Sister's condition. They could hear the two talking but could not understand what they were saying.

Mr. Hudson tried to chat with the stranger but the latter did not seem to want to talk. Then Papa came out of the bedroom, shaking his head.

"You'll have to excuse me, sir, but we have a sick little daughter. She fell out in the barn and hit her head on the manger. We're worried about her." He looked directly at the man. "And your name. . . ."

"Aaron Carter. I arrived just before the storm hit."

Carolyn stared at him and wondered why he was so interested in the poison ring.

The man went on. "Have you had a doctor for your daughter?"

Papa shook his head. "We haven't because in this part of the country it isn't possible to call one in. Now with this bad weather we can't get her to Spokane to see one. It was a nasty fall. She was unconscious for almost two days. We are praying that she will be all right soon."

The man seemed to be thinking. At last he said, "I'm a doctor. Perhaps I can help."

Papa looked sharply at him, then said, "I'll tell my wife." He turned and went back into the bedroom.

Carolyn could not take her eyes from the stranger as he sat staring at the table where the box of jewelry had been sitting. Was he thinking of the poison ring?

Papa stepped to the bedroom door and looked at the man. "Will you come in, please? You may be able to give us some idea of how the child really is."

Carolyn followed him as far as the bedroom door where she could look into the room and see him beginning to examine Frances. He was leaning over the trundle bed until Papa shoved a chair toward him and he sat down.

He gently felt Little Sister's head and looked closely into her eyes, then examined the small neck and shoulders. His hands carefully went back to her head and when Frances winced, he said, "That hurts, doesn't it, my little one?"

She glanced at Mama, then began to cry. Dr. Carter

leaned back in his chair and stared thoughtfully at her as Mama came over and took Frances' small hand in hers. She brushed back loose hair from the small forehead.

"I'm afraid your daughter has a concussion," he said slowly.

At the word "concussion" Mama drew in her breath sharply.

Dr. Carter went on carefully, "She will have headaches and trouble with her eyes for a while. And possibly dizzy spells."

Mama said, "Will she get over it? What can we do for her?"

"It was evidently a bad fall, but I'm sure she will recover. Do you have anything to help her with pain? The headaches may be bad at times."

"We have laudanum for emergencies but I don't think I would give it to a child." Papa shook his head.

"No," said Dr. Carter thoughtfully, "unless you gave her a very small amount in water, say about a fourth of a teaspoonful. You might try it next time her head hurts too much and see how she reacts."

Papa did not say anything more, but he apparently was wondering if they dare follow this doctor's suggestion. As he stepped out of the bedroom he said shortly, "We'll see."

Carolyn felt her parents would rather have had the diagnosis of a regular doctor.

Mama came our right behind Papa and went to the cupboard.

"Where in the world did I put that thermometer?"

She began searching on one of the shelves. "It should be here." She looked around. "Dr. Carter wants to take Little Sister's temperature. Oh, there it is!"

She quickly reached for it and returned to the bedroom.

By the time Mama came back with the thermometer Little Sister had gone to sleep and the doctor was sitting quietly watching her. He did not bother to take her temperature then but returned to the kitchen-living room. Then he left, saying he hoped to see them again soon.

At last Carolyn told Papa and Mama she was sure that was the man who had been watching her and the children make snow angels.

The next day Frances was up for a few minutes trying to walk around. She kept getting dizzy and would have to sit down or fall down. Soon Mama took the little girl back to the trundle bed and tucked her in. She kissed her as soon as she was asleep, and returned to the rest of the family.

She said, "We must pray harder. All things are possible to them who love the Lord. We must have faith that she is going to be all right."

She turned to Mrs. Hudson. "Before you leave for your own cabin, I want to explain about the poison ring and how it was used. Noblemen used to wear them filled with poison because if an enemy wanted to capture or kill the man he could always end his own life. Or he could put poison into tea or coffee of an enemy and kill him. Since coming to America,

I have had the feeling that in those early days men had a peculiar sense of justice."

"Oh, Mama! How awful!" Carolyn had never heard this about the ring.

"Just a minute," said Mama, turning. "I'll get the ring again."

She went into the bedroom and soon returned with the box and carefully put it on the table.

"I've had the things in this box for so long I guess I act too protective of it. Some of the things came to America with my family from Denmark when I was only fourteen. I don't remember much about Denmark anymore because now my home is in America, but I think some of these things are rather valuable."

As Mama opened the box Carolyn immediately noticed that the ring in its little bag was not on top. That was odd. She was sure that Mama had laid it on top of everything instead of putting it way back in one corner as she usually did. The stranger had been drinking his coffee and Little Sister had started crying. Mama certainly had not been her usual self right then.

As Mama talked she was taking the things out of the box and making a small pile on the table. Finally she reached into the corner where she usually kept the ring in its little string purse.

Suddenly, her hand in the act of reaching, she became very quiet. Carolyn saw a puzzled look come into her eyes and with both hands she began probing every corner of the box. Then slowly she began to spread everything out on the table.

Carolyn and Mrs. Hudson looked at each other and both began to frown.

"Mama, is something the matter? Are you all right?"

Mama's face had gone white!

"The ring is gone," she whispered. Then she said louder, "How could that be? None of you children have ever been allowed into this box unless I've been with you. Papa never has as far as I know. How *could* it be gone?"

"Mama, don't you remember you put the ring on top of everything the last time you put it away? Dr. Carter had just come in."

"Even so, it should be here," she answered, once more going over the jewelry spread out on the table. Now she stood gripping her hands as Papa and Mr. Hudson, followed by Eddie and Robert David, came into the room.

"Philip! My ring is gone! The poison ring!" Mama's voice broke. "I—I don't see how it could be, but it is!"

Papa frowned. "You're sure?" He walked over and looked down at everything spread over the table. Then he looked at each child, but he knew without asking that none of them had taken it.

Robert David and Sally Mae looked first at Mama and then at Papa, then at their own parents, their eyes wide and questioning. Carolyn looked Papa in the eyes. She certainly had not taken it.

Mrs. Hudson put a hand on Robert David's shoulder. "Son, have either you or Sally Mae been in Mrs. Standar's box?"

He shook his head. "I don't even know where she kept it. I've never been in the bedroom." He turned suddenly to Sally Mae. "Have you?"

Sally Mae, her eyes big, said, "Only to see Frances. I didn't know where the ring was."

"No, I guess neither of you have," said Mrs. Hudson, relief sounding in her voice.

Everyone was quiet for a few moments. There was simply no way the ring should be gone—but it was!

Mama said, "I guess the ring was valuable because of the gold in it, but to me it was valuable in a much more important way. It was through an aunt of mine who was lady-in-waiting to the Queen of Denmark that I met Christian Hamilton, the nobleman who asked me to marry him. That ring was part of my past so I've cherished it."

"Say!" Papa broke in. "That strange man was in this room for a few minutes, *alone,* yesterday when he was here. Remember when you were looking for the thermometer? I had just come out and was sitting here at the table, but he was still with Frances." Papa never called her "Frances" unless he was upset.

"Oh, Philip!" Mama wrung her hands. "Surely—surely—I don't see how he had time to get that ring, to dig down into the corner of the box. I was out such a short time."

Carolyn looked sharply at her mother. "But, Mama, you didn't put it in the corner the last time! You put it on top of everything. Don't you remember?"

Mama frowned, trying to remember. She shook her head. "Maybe you're right. I've been so upset over Little Sister's condition."

Then Carolyn added, "Mama, that man stared at the ring when he first came into the house. I thought he acted as though he recognized it. Anyway, he acted funny—I mean, he acted oddly, but I thought you noticed."

"I noticed him simply because he reminded me of someone I knew in Denmark. It's been so long, he has changed. He was a man I never did like. He was a friend of Christian's but I never trusted him."

She shook her head. "I don't think I noticed him looking at the ring. I've been too worried about other things. I just thought he looked familiar and I couldn't think why."

She continued to stare at the jewelry spread out on the table.

"Whatever can we do? That ring means a lot to me."

Carolyn's heart ached. Mama looked as though she wanted to cry.

Papa, standing near her, put an arm over her shoulders and pulled her close to him.

"Does the ring matter that much anymore, my Louisa? Surely our lives here and our family must mean more to you now."

Mama took a deep breath and swallowed hard. She brushed one hand across her forehead and turned and laid her head on Papa's shoulder.

Carolyn barely heard her muffled reply. "Of course, Philip! You're right. That ring is something out of the past. Maybe this is God's way of telling me to think only of the present. It's Little Sister and all of you who need my attention now."

She threw both arms around Papa's neck and he held her close.

What would happen next about the ring?

SIXTEEN

THE MYSTERY DEEPENS

The next day, bright and early, three of the uncles arrived to help the Hudsons go home. Jake was carrying two pairs of barrel-stave skis for the parents. Louie was carrying two pairs of very short ones for Robert David and Sally Mae. Will was pulling the little sled that Papa had given the children. This would be for Merrilee to ride in.

Adolph had stayed behind to dig out enough of the packed snow so the Hudsons could get into their cabin, since they had not been at home during the blizzard.

Mrs. Hudson seemed overcome at all the help although she had become used to the Standar families helping. She could never forget how the Standars had taken them into their home and helped them get settled when they first arrived.

Louie put a pair of the short skis on the floor.

"Here, Robert David! Do you think you can walk on these?" He was grinning. "I'll help you. It may not be easy at first."

Robert David cautiously put his feet into the binding, then Louie wrapped a long leather strap around his foot and ankle. As Louie was tying it, Sally Mae stepped into hers and just stood waiting. She kept glancing down at her feet.

Mrs. Hudson looked amused and a bit uncertain. "If anyone needs help, I'm afraid I am the one. I've never been on skis before."

"None of us has," said Mr. Hudson, "but I certainly am willing to give it a try."

"We'll go outside before putting the skis on the rest of you," said Louie, lifting Robert David, skis and all, and stepping to the door. "I just wanted to see how these fit."

As Louie was helping Robert David to the top of the snowbank, Mr. Hudson picked up Sally Mae and the skis and everyone trooped outside.

Everyone except Carolyn. She stooped down to pick up the little lamb nuzzling around her long skirt. She picked up her slate and went into the bedroom to tell Mama, sitting with Frances, that the Hudsons were leaving and she would sit with Little Sister if Mama wanted to say good-bye.

"Thank you, dear," said Mama, getting up and going out of the room as Carolyn put the slate down on the covers.

Then she laid the lamb on Little Sister's bed, and the latter held out a slim hand to pet it. Carolyn could tell she did not feel very well, but she hoped the lamb would help bring back a sparkle to the eyes that were no longer laughing. She watched for a moment, then leaned over to kiss the little girl on the forehead.

Now Carolyn settled her slate on one knee and began to sketch a picture of the man who called himself Dr. Carter. If she could get it as she wanted, like the man himself, she would draw it on paper so it could be shown to people. She was hardly aware of the Hudsons leaving.

Carolyn liked to draw. She had drawn pictures of each member of the family, which her mother carefully saved. Mrs. Standar was not surprised that she had a daughter who liked to draw, since she herself had once wanted to draw portraits. But her life had been much too busy.

When Mama and her older brother, Edward, had left Denmark with their parents so long ago, they had been very poor after the family had been robbed of that money and lost everything. After their father died, both Mama and her brother had gone to work, Mama as a domestic and Edward on a farm at one dollar a day, in order to support the family. Carolyn remembered Mama telling all this.

Mama would say, "No matter how poor you are, never forget God. He will help you through bad times and good. In the noisy confusion of life, always keep peace with God and your soul."

Carolyn was not exactly sure what she meant by "keeping peace with God and your soul," but maybe it meant to always do right and help people.

To Carolyn the world was a beautiful place, here in this Big Bend Basin near the Columbia River. When the sun shown or the moon and the stars came out at night, it was breathtaking.

Mama once told her that she had not liked living in such a big crowded city as New York. She could still remember her confusion when they had arrived from Denmark, a confusion of life that made the entire family unhappy. But now Mama thought the whole world was beautiful, and she was right.

Carolyn finished the sketch of Dr. Carter, then put the slate to one side to copy it onto paper later. Now she would draw something to entertain Little Sister. She reached for a piece of wrapping paper.

She began to recite the nursery rhyme *Mary Had a Little Lamb* as she drew a picture of a small lamb.

" 'Its fleece was white as snow.' "

"What is 'fleece'?" asked Frances, patting the lamb's head.

"You're patting it," said Carolyn. "It's the woolie coat on the little lamb." She was drawing a little girl.

" 'And everywhere that Mary went, her lamb was sure to go.' "

She made a lamb beside Mary, both walking toward a schoolhouse.

" 'He followed her to school one day, which was against the rule.' "

Then she made some children playing with the lamb.

" 'It made the children laugh and play, to see a lamb at school.' "

Just then Carolyn heard someone catch a breath at her shoulder. She glanced up to see Mama staring down at the sketch on the slate.

"Are the Hudsons gone?" asked Carolyn.

Her mother nodded, then said, "I can't believe it! When I saw Dr. Carter, he reminded me of someone. Your sketch looks like the man I mentioned, that I knew in Denmark years ago. He's older now, of course. I did not like him."

As she kept staring at the picture, Carolyn said to Frances, "No more now, honey. We'll do some more later."

She looked up at her mother. "You knew that man, Mama?"

"If it's who I think it is, yes." She sounded puzzled. "I'm just not sure."

Papa came into the bedroom. "Now that everyone is gone, it'll be lonesome around here."

He bent over the trundle bed. "How's my girl?" he kissed her gently on one cheek and patted the head of the little lamb still cuddled in Frances' arms.

"My head hurts," she said. "That mean old manger doesn't like me. Kiss the lamb?"

Papa's eyes twinkled. "No, I'll let you kiss it."

Just then Carolyn thrust the sketches she had made of Mary and her lamb into Little Sister's hand and smiled at her.

"Here, you may have these. We'll finish the whole poem later."

Papa glanced at the picture of Dr. Carter on the slate.

"Ummm, a good likeness. How about making some drawings on paper? Maybe two or three copies. I'll carry them with me when I go out and see if anyone knows where he is staying."

"Like the time I drew those pictures of the men who robbed the Spokane bank?" asked Carolyn.

"Exactly!" Papa smiled, remembering how Carolyn's sketches had helped in catching the robbers. "Nice to have an artist in the family. She takes after you, my Louisa," he said as he gave Mama a hug.

"I'll go out to the kitchen table," said Carolyn, gathering up her slate and sketching things.

"Shall I take the lamb?" She looked down at Little Sister.

"No." The latter kept one arm around the baby lamb. "It likes me. Does it have a name?"

"Yes, Icicle. Icicle Baby."

Papa looked amused. "Isn't that an odd name for a newborn lamb?"

Carolyn smiled. "Well, I couldn't think of anything except she was born during that freezing weather and was cold and white as an icicle."

Eddie stepped in just in time to hear her. He grunted. "Icicles aren't white. They're clear as water because they *are* water, frozen water dripping from the eaves."

"I don't care," said Carolyn. "I like 'Icicle.' My Icicle Baby." She gave the lamb a pat as it lay quietly in Little Sister's arms, touching its nose to her cheek.

"I like 'Icicle' too," said the little girl softly. She held her cheek against the tiny head. "Dear little Icy."

"Out you go," said Mama firmly. "If the girls want to name the lamb 'Icicle,' I guess it's none of our business." She gave Eddie a gentle shove toward the door. "How about bringing in some wood?"

Carolyn had finished her drawings of Dr. Carter by the time Eddie returned.

"Say, you know what? It's warming up." He dropped the wood in the woodbox, took off his jacket, and hung it on one of the pegs near the stove. "Chinook, I'll bet."

Papa looked up from the book he was reading. "I thought it felt warmer when I was out this morning." He put the book back on a small shelf near his chair. "I think we'd better get out and check the animals. If a chinook wind starts melting the snow too fast, we are apt to be surrounded by water."

Eddie looked at Carolyn. "Sis, if some of this snow disappears, it may be a good time to examine that cave where we saw the smoke when we were out looking for Spots. Want to go? We'll wait another day. I'm going to find out what was causing that smoke."

"Sure," said Carolyn, always ready for adventure with brother Eddie. "I'll be ready when you are."

SEVENTEEN

A CHINOOK HELPS SOLVE THE MYSTERY

Two days later the two older children were able to reach the Coulee wall overlooking the huge Steamboat Rock looming up from the middle of the Coulee floor. Carolyn could see pools of water standing near the high landmark. It had not taken long for the warm chinook wind to melt the deep snow. Great banks of it were disappearing fast.

When she had asked Papa what a chinook wind meant, Papa said it was a current of air warmed by the Japanese current that swept over the mountains from the west. It became warmer and drier and as it reached eastern Washington Territory it melted the snow very rapidly, sometimes in only a few days.

It did indeed melt the snow fast. Eddie was riding Spots and Carolyn was riding her pony Flame, whose coat was a shining reddish brown in the bright sunshine. The horses squished along in the melted snow, bare ground showing instead of the deep snow that had been there only a few days earlier.

That morning at sunrise a red glow deepened the sky as though trying to see how fast the snow would melt. The earth was almost bare in spots, with what looked like little piles of hay scattered around. Then Carolyn realized it was bunchgrass that, during the past summer, had been growing tall and lush. Now it was dry and bunched over in small clumps. This was the wild hay that range cattle ate during the winter, after pawing through the snow to get at it.

Then things began to show up that were not so pleasant. A few dead cows and horses were lying on their sides, bloated, with legs sticking straight out in the air.

"Oh," said Carolyn sadly. "I don't like to see that."

"No," Eddie agreed. "I don't either. It means the critters couldn't dig down through the deep snow to get at the grass, and the cold was so intense it killed them. Winter isn't very pleasant for animals sometimes."

The two rode on, dodging pools of water formed from the melting snow.

Then Carolyn pointed to one side at a mound higher than the surrounding area. "Look!" Two small bedraggled animals stood chattering near an opening in the ground. Then another little head popped up.

"Gophers," said Eddie. "Water in their homes. Lots of them will drown."

As the children neared the Coulee wall buzzards

were flying everywhere, some high in the sky, some close to the ground.

"Dead cows or horses down over the wall, I'll bet." Eddie was looking up into the sky. "Coyotes and mountain lions will eat the meat but the scavenger buzzards will pick the bones clean."

"I don't like to think about it," said Carolyn quietly. After that she tried not to look at the many dead animals.

It was hard not to look, however, after they reached the Coulee wall. The animals, lost in the heavy blizzard with its terrible wind forcing them farther and farther toward the Coulee, had fallen over the edge to die. Now the bodies were scattered down the 800-foot wall. In some areas the wall was almost straight up and down and nothing could stick. In other spots the wall was slanting enough that rock ledges held the now dead animals.

"I wish I hadn't seen this," said Carolyn. "I don't like to see all these poor dead creatures and think of what they suffered."

"I don't like it either," said Eddie, "but this is what can happen to range stock. We're lucky we were able to keep our cattle fenced in and that we found our ponies."

They were riding along the edge of the bench land toward the area where they had found Spots, King, and Nell earlier, but they were not sure where they had seen the rising smoke. Everything and every place looked so different with so much of the snow gone.

With nothing turning green yet, the country was not pretty as it would be later in the spring. Carolyn tried to watch the clouds, soft and white and fluffy along the horizon, and to enjoy the silence, which could be peaceful and restful. She just would not look at the death around her.

Two magpies, black and white birds with long, slim tails, flew across her line of vision just as Eddie held up one hand. Their ponies stopped and stood still. "Listen! I think I hear someone talking."

Sure enough! Very, very faintly Carolyn too heard voices, loud and then too soft to distinguish, then loud again. They could not understand what was being said.

Carolyn looked all around. "Who is it? *Where* is it?"

Eddie shook his head. "I don't know unless it is in one of those small caves along the face of this part of the Coulee wall. There's a place father along where we can crawl down. I don't want to take the ponies though. Come on." He jerked his head forward.

Kicking Flame gently, Carolyn continued to follow Eddie on Spots and wondered who could be living in one of those small caves.

It was not long before the voices became louder. Whoever was talking had to be in one of the small caves.

Eddie slipped off his pony, threw the reins over Spots' head, and let them "tie" to the ground. He walked slowly over toward the edge of the big shelf of land they had been riding on.

He looked over, then beckoned to Carolyn. She

did the same with her reins, and as Flame stood still she ran to Eddie's side.

The voices seemed to be coming from underneath. Below must be a cave, although from where they stood they could not see anything.

Eddie pointed to a narrow path. "There's the way they get into the cave. Guess we might as well go down."

Carolyn's neck felt prickly at the thought of going down, but Eddie was already moving forward, so she followed.

They had no idea what to expect, then without any warning they came to the small opening into the cave.

Inside, arguing, were Dr. Carter and Jens Hamilton. What in the world were they doing here and together?

"Let me have that, you fool!" Jens was saying roughly. "You had no right to steal it!"

"All right—but what will you do with it?"

Dr. Carter started to hold out and open his clenched fist, then changed his mind. Jens grabbed for it as he started to jerk it back.

Something fell to the stony floor of the cave. The children were amazed to see Mama's poison ring fall and roll over, then lie quietly.

Carolyn gasped and ran past Eddie to snatch up the ring.

"Neither one of you can have this!" she said fiercely. "What do you think you're doing with this? Mama has been almost sick about it being gone." She glared at Dr. Carter. "This is Mama's ring."

The men stared first at Carolyn, and then at Eddie.

Finally Dr. Carter said, "No, it isn't. It belongs to the Royal House of Denmark."

Eddie stood by without saying anything. There was something here he did not understand. Then he said quietly to Carolyn, "Maybe we'd better let the men explain." He looked at them. "Mama has had that ring for a long, long time. Why do you say it isn't hers?"

Jens sighed. "Ditlef is right," he said softly. Carolyn and Eddie looked at Dr. Carter in surprise.

"Ditlef?" Carolyn echoed. Dr. Carter sighed and nodded.

"My name is Ditlef Carsten, not Aaron Carter. I am Herman Carsten's half-brother. I came to American to find your family and try to make up for the damage Herman caused. When I discovered Jens was here too, I realized he was searching for the ring. Then I saw the ring at your house and I took it, without even really thinking about it. I acted out of impulse . . . the loss of part of our royal treasury was a blow to all of us in Denmark."

"You see," Jens said quietly, "the ring belongs to the Royal House. It should never have left the country. My brother was so in love with your mother that he was not thinking clearly when he gave it to her. Then your mother's family left the country, and it was too late to get it back. I decided to visit America one day, and find your mother so I could ask her to let me return the ring to the Royal House." He paused and glanced at Ditlef. "I just wish I had known Ditlef was coming here too. We could have avoided many problems by coming together."

Carolyn did not know what to do, but she was *not* giving up the ring. She stood glaring at the men until finally Eddie said, "Why don't we all go home and see what Mama has to say about it?"

Jens seemed to welcome that suggestion. He nodded. "Yes, a good idea. I have to see her anyway. I'm sure she will understand. Ditlef should not have taken it as he did. He could have told me and we could have talked with your folks about it."

He looked at the other man and Ditlef glanced down as though he was somewhat ashamed.

"All I could think of was getting the ring back," he said slowly. Now he looked up. "I guess you're right, but I don't need to go. You people go ahead and explain to your mother about it."

"Oh, yes, you do need to go!" said Jens quickly. "You're not going to get out of this that easily. Let's go! Our horses are down the trail. Where are yours?"

"On top," said Eddie. "We'll go ahead and you can follow us later."

Mama and Papa had a hard time understanding what had happened when Eddie and Carolyn showed the ring and tried to tell them about finding the men in the cave.

When the two men arrived they all sat down and listened again as Jens and Ditlef each explained their reasons for wanting to find the Standar family.

"But what were you doing staying in that cave?" Mama asked Jens, still confused. He smiled sheepishly.

"I wanted to learn more about this country, about cowboys and Indians. I thought that if I camped out in that cave, I would understand their way of life better. It seemed especially convenient, since it was fairly close to your home. However, I did not plan on running into blizzard conditions, or so much snow."

"How did Ditlef know you were there?" Papa asked curiously.

"I saw Jens a few days ago and followed him to the cave," Ditlef explained. "He didn't even realize I was here until I came to the cave today with the ring. When he found out that I'd stolen it, he wanted to bring it back to you and explain. By that time I realized I'd done a foolish thing, and I was afraid you would think I was stealing from you like Herman had. So I didn't want to come back. That's what the children heard us fighting about."

Mama shook her head, still trying to take it all in.

"Of course I didn't know that ring was not supposed to leave the Royal family," she said. "To me it was just something with which to remember Christian. My folks were having so much trouble about then, what with Herman stealing the money and my father not being very well. He needed that money so desperately that I think it broke his heart. All I could think about, of course, was having to leave Christian."

Ditlef quietly reached into his pocket and said, "This is why I came to America, to find you and to give you this." He held out a long envelope. "I just returned from Spokane where I had this in safekeeping with the bank. Now I can go home, knowing the old debt is happily settled."

Puzzled, Mama took the envelope and slowly opened it.

She had sent Eddie over to get Grandma and Grandpa and they came in just as she was pulling something from the envelope.

She gasped and said, "Oh, no, not this much!" She held up a bank draft for $3,500, then handed it to Grandma.

"You forget," said Ditlef gently, "that the original $1,000 has been collecting interest all these years."

Grandma handed the draft to Grandpa without saying anything except, "How different our lives would have been if this had been in our hands thirty years ago."

She then said something to Jens in Danish. He smiled and replied in Danish, then in English he said, "She's sorry I am leaving because now she won't have anyone to talk with in Danish."

Grandpa handed the draft to Papa, who looked at it, then handed it back to Mama.

"But—but—" Mama couldn't seem to go on.

"It's yours," said Ditlef, smiling. "The estate has waited a long time to get this settled. If there hadn't been so much snow I would have had this in your hands sooner. Also I had to be sure you were the right parties. The ring proved that."

They talked a little longer. The ring was lying on

the table before them and no one was paying any attention to it.

Carolyn wondered how her mother really felt about it now that she knew it should not have left the Royal House. It seemed so odd that such a simple thing as a ring could have caused so much trouble.

Finally, preparing to leave, the men arose from the table. Papa and Grandpa shook hands with each, thanking them for all the trouble they had gone to in order to return the money.

Papa said, "We can never really thank you enough. This money will help our children get through school, and provide some extra to have on hand for our parents' use. And I hope we can use some to get help for our little daughter as soon as we can get her to the doctor in Spokane." He held up both hands. "Now may the peace of God, which passeth all understanding, keep your hearts through Jesus Christ, our Lord."

"Amen," said Grandpa and Grandma together.

Tears were running down Mama's cheeks. She normally was not an impulsive person, but now she stepped to the table, picked up the ring, turned and placed it in Jens' hand, then kissed him on one cheek.

"Tell Christian for me that I hope he is as happily married as I am, with as fine a family as I have. Please take the ring and return it to wherever it belongs. I've cherished it long enough. God bless all of you."

She walked over and stood beside Papa. He put one arm around her and held her close, then they walked to the door with the two men as they left.

Carolyn and Eddie looked at each other. They knew that the amazing story of their mother's early life had a happy ending, and that they and Little Sister were a part of it.

God in his great goodness had made everything come out just right.